Yobgorgle

Who or what is Yobgorgle?

Eugene Winkleman, who is visiting
Rochester, New York, with his Uncle Mel,
first learns about Yobgorgle when he goes to
see a documentary movie about the mysterious monster that is supposed to live in
nearby Lake Ontario.

The movie shows all sorts of people who
claim to have encountered Yobgorgle. One
of them, Professor Ambrose McFwain of the
Piscean Discovery Institute in Rochester,
says he thinks he heard Yobgorgle clearly on
a hydrophone. It sounded like a 1956 Chevy
with bad valves.

Since Eugene doesn't have anything special to do in Rochester, he decides to call the
Professor and offer to help him with his
monster-hunting. Little does Eugene know
that his offer will involve him and Uncle
Mel in a wild midnight voyage with the Professor in search of the mystery monster.

What Eugene and the other crew members discover that night leads to a climax
that's as zany as it is exciting.

Fans of such other books by Daniel Pinkwater as *Lizard Music* and *The Last Guru*
will agree that *Yobgorgle* ranks among his
funniest and most original novels.

Also by Daniel M. Pinkwater
(with Jill Pinkwater)

SUPERPUPPY
*How to Choose, Raise and Train
the Best Possible Dog for You*

Yobgorgle

MYSTERY MONSTER OF LAKE ONTARIO

...

by Daniel M. Pinkwater

 Houghton Mifflin/Clarion Books/New York

Library of Congress Cataloging in Publication Data

Pinkwater, Daniel Manus, 1941–
Yobgorgle, mystery monster of Lake Ontario.

"A Clarion book."
SUMMARY: While visiting Rochester, New York, young Eugene meets the strange Professor Ambrose McFwain and goes out with him in his boat to search for a mysterious sea monster that has been sighted on Lake Ontario.
[1.   Sea monsters—Fiction]   I.   Title.
PZ7.P6335Yo   [Fic]   79-11364   ISBN 0-395-28970-X

· 1 ·

This is about the time I lived for two weeks in a motel in Rochester, New York, with my Uncle Mel, and what happened to me while I was there.

My parents had gone to Europe for six weeks. They had been talking about going since before I was born. My mother always said they would never really go. She said they just talked about it, but they never went. She said probably I'd be all grown up, and they'd be old and gray before they ever took a trip to Europe. Then they won a contest! My mother cut a coupon out of a newspaper, and sent it in with a label from

1

a jar of low-calorie, low-cholesterol, imitation chicken fat, and they won the grand prize—six weeks in fourteen European countries, all expenses paid, deluxe air-conditioned buses, meals and tips included—for two. The second prize was a home video-tape machine. I would have liked it better if they had won that, because I could have started a collection of science-fiction movies. But they won the trip, and off they went—and off I went, to spend six weeks with my Uncle Mel.

Which was not so bad. Uncle Mel isn't married, and he lives in an apartment about two blocks away from our house in Cliffside Park, New Jersey. So really nothing would be changed—I'd see my same friends and do all the same things. The only difference would be that I'd live with my Uncle Mel, which meant that I could stay up late and have pizza and hamburgers just about every day. Also, Uncle Mel goes skeet shooting on weekends, and he said that he would take me with him and let me shoot his shotgun. So it promised to be a pretty good summer. And my parents had promised to bring me all kinds of good souvenirs from Europe. It would have been better, of course, if they'd won the video-tape machine—but you can't have it all your way.

Then Uncle Mel found out that he was going to have to go to Rochester, New York, for two weeks to take a course. He has a job selling and installing these food vending machines. They have ones that sell coffee, and ones that sell ice cream, and ones that sell sandwiches, and lately, ones with little micro-wave ovens in them, so you can get a hot corned-beef sandwich wrapped in cellophane, or a frankfurter. Uncle Mel's company wanted him to go to Rochester, New York, to learn to operate a new type of machine that has freeze-dried chemical foods in it. When you push the button, after depositing your coins, the freeze-dried food, which is in little cellophane envelopes, gets water injected into the envelope, and then it gets mushed around, and then it gets micro-waved. It all comes from space technology. So if you wanted, say, a bowl of chili with crackers, you'd deposit your coins, push the button for chili with crackers, and this cellophane envelope of reddish powder that has a shelf-life of sixty years, without refrigeration, gets injected, mixed, mushed, micro-waved, and served up in a little styrofoam cup. Same thing with the crackers.

Uncle Mel lives on nothing but junk food. On his *birthday* he eats a Greaso-Whammy burger from McTavish's—that's his favorite fast-food chain. He hasn't eaten anything off a real plate in years—just cardboard and plastic—and even *he* can't stand the stuff that comes out of those machines. He says he doesn't know who eats it. Nobody knows, he says. They just come around every couple of months to fill up the machines, and some of the stuff has been sold.

Anyway, the new freeze-dried, mix, mush and micro-wave machine was supposed to be real complicated, and Uncle Mel was going to have to go up to Rochester, New York, where the factory is, and take a two-week course in how the thing was put together, and how to fix it, and how to work it. The company was going to pay all the expenses, his room, train fare, meals—the whole works.

Since my parents had already left when Uncle Mel got the news, he decided that he'd better take me along. "Eugene," he said, "have you ever wanted to see Rochester, New York?" I told him that it wasn't a place I had always longed to see—but I hadn't traveled much, and I was in favor of the idea. Uncle Mel said that was good, because I didn't have any choice anyhow.

We took the train. Uncle Mel said it was so

that I could see the country. That was a lie. Actually, Uncle Mel is deathly afraid of airplanes, ever since he cut himself with one of those little plastic knives with serrated edges they give you with your meal on airplanes. Also, he hates airplane food. On the train, they have a sort of fast-food counter, and you can get a micro-waved hamburger or a powdered scrambled-egg sandwich. Uncle Mel gets nervous when he doesn't have access to junk food. The fact is, the stuff they give you on airplanes is too classy for him.

The train ride was pretty good. We sat right next to the fast-food section, and by the time we got to Rochester, Uncle Mel had tried everything they had. The trip was supposed to take seven hours, but it took nine because they were repairing the tracks. Uncle Mel decided that the best thing they served was micro-waved hot pastrami on a rye roll. He made notes about the junk food in a little book he always carries. Uncle Mel says that the best thing that can happen to you is to be really interested in your work. As a natural glutton and junk-food junkie, Uncle Mel is truly a happy man with the job he has.

I enjoyed the train ride. For a long time we

ran right along the Hudson River. The conduc-
tor came through every now and then and told
things about the places we were passing. He'd
read up on the history of every place his train
passed. He'd tell us that the big house on the
right was built by colonel so-and-so in
eighteen-oh-eight, and he died and left it to his
sister, who married Mr. Such-and-such, and
later it was bought by the famous Whooziz fam-
ily who built the railroad.

It was interesting to listen to what the con-
ductor said and look out the window. We went
through a lot of forests and farmland and passed
through little old-looking towns. I had brought
a lot of comic books with me to read on the trip,
but I didn't read one. I just looked out the window and felt the rocking and rumbling of the
train and counted the number of sandwiches
Uncle Mel ate. He had eleven. There were nine
kinds of sandwiches offered on the train, and he
had two extra micro-waved hot pastramis on rye
rolls.

It was getting dark when we arrived in
Rochester. We went straight to the motel. I
couldn't tell much about the city from the taxi
ride from the station. In the motel, I checked
out the color TV while Uncle Mel went out to

look for a fast-food place. He came back with a bunch of Greaso-Whammies in a paper bag, and some milk shakes. I ate a Greaso-Whammy. Uncle Mel ate three. Then we watched a movie about cowboys and went to sleep.

· 2 ·

It was hot. It was already eighty-two degrees in Rochester when Uncle Mel and I went to McTavish's for breakfast. We both had eggs McTavish—a poached egg with olives and cheese on a taco shell. I had a cola. Uncle Mel had coffee. Then he asked me if I knew how to get back to the motel, gave me two dollars for lunch, told me he'd be back to take me out to supper at about six-thirty, and left for the factory where they make Mix-and-Mush Micro-Wave Food Vendors.

I finished my cola and thought about what I'd like to do for the rest of the day. People were going to work, stopping into McTavish's for a fast breakfast. They got on and off of buses. Everybody looked sort of bleary-eyed, as though they hadn't slept well during the hot night. I went out into the street. There were a lot of tall buildings and people hurrying. The sun was bright. The sidewalks had this glittery stuff mixed in with the concrete, so that it was uncomfortable to keep your eyes down and uncomfortable to keep your eyes up. The day was going to be a scorcher, there was no doubt about it.

I wandered around the downtown area for a while. I looked in store windows and at the buildings. They were just buildings—nice, I suppose, but nothing very interesting. The best building in Rochester is this parking garage where the cars park on spiral ramps. The whole thing looks like it's screwed into the ground. I wondered if they could really make a building like that. When it got full of cars, they could just unscrew it a turn, and expose another level. There were two or three movie houses—I had considered going to a movie to get into the air-conditioning—but none of them were showing movies that a kid is allowed to see.

There was this underground thing, a sort of

mall, I suppose, in the basement of one of the big office buildings. It had stores in it, and a weird thing like a clock or a sculpture that rotated slowly, and there were these cylinders that went around, and every hour they were supposed to open and you could see dolls representing different countries inside. It was altogether the dumbest-looking thing I've ever seen. Also in the underground mall there was a great big scale model of the White House on display—like a giant doll house. People were lined up to see it. It was sort of nice, I guess. I wasn't very interested. The only nice thing about the mall was that it was air-conditioned.

I walked around for a while, but I didn't see anybody my age—at least not on their own. There were kids with their mothers, going shopping, or going to the doctor—that sort of thing. Cliffside Park isn't far from New York City. You can see New York City across the river from some streets in Cliffside Park, and there's a bus that goes there—but I'm not allowed to go by myself. If I go to New York City, it's with some responsible adult, and it's on serious business of some kind. I don't get to hang out and meet any other kids. It was just the same in downtown Rochester. I hadn't really thought about it before I came, but it seemed entirely possible that I was going to be mostly alone for the whole two weeks.

I got tired of walking around the mall and went outside into the street. It was really hot! I looked at a clock on a building, and saw that it wasn't even ten o'clock yet. People were going to be falling dead from the heat before the day was over. I discovered that I was slightly lost. That wasn't much of a problem—just a matter of getting my bearings. There's a river running right through the middle of Rochester. It's called the Genesee River. It isn't much of a river compared to, say, the Hudson, but it makes it pretty much impossible to get lost in the middle of town. The motel we were staying at, a blue and white building, was right near the river.

After I found the river, I decided I'd go back to the motel. I was hot and bored. At least the motel room would be cool. I thought I might have a look at the comic books I had taken along on the train, and not read.

I'm a fairly fast reader, and it wasn't long before I finished all the comics. I had the TV running the whole time and flicked from channel to channel—there wasn't anything on. I made a trip to the soda machine, and the ice machine. I took a shower. It got to be noon. Lunch—that was something to do. I went outside to look for a place to eat. I didn't want to go to McTavish's because that was most likely where Uncle Mel was going to want to have supper. This trip to Rochester was turning out to be one big bore.

I thought that maybe I could get a model airplane kit to build in the motel room. That would keep me busy for a while. I had noticed a hobby section in a big department store I had walked through that morning. The truth is, I'm not all that crazy about building models—it's something I usually do when I'm sick in bed or there's absolutely nobody around to hang out with. I figured that I could probably put together at least twenty-five models while I was in Rochester. I thought about all this while I was walking around looking for a place to have lunch.

In among the modern buildings in downtown Rochester are some streets with real old buildings. I like the old buildings better than the new ones. They're smaller and darker and sort of friendlier. The new ones all look sort of dumb—except the spiral garage—I was getting to like that one better every time I saw it. In one of the streets with old buildings, I found a place called Bob's Beanery. It had a counter and stools and a tile floor and little hand-lettered signs all over the front of it telling what they had to eat that day. One of the signs said

BOB'S LAKE ONTARIO CHILI 65¢
SECOND BOWL FREE—
—CRACKERS AND BEVERAGE INCLUDED.

That looked liked the best deal in the place. I studied the rest of the signs and couldn't find anything else that cheap. I went inside, climbed onto a counter stool, and asked for a bowl of Lake Ontario chili. I found out why they call it Lake Ontario chili. It was pretty watery. But it didn't taste too bad. I had the free second bowl, and a cola with it. There was one of those big electric fans in the place, the kind that stands on the floor and turns from side to side. Every time it turned in my direction it made little ripples on the surface of my Lake Ontario chili.

After lunch, I headed back toward the motel. I just couldn't think of anything else to do. This time I was walking on the opposite side of the street—the river side. Across this street, opposite the motel, was a big gray building. I hadn't paid much attention to it—I figured it was a post office or something like that. Now I noticed that it was the public library. I went up the stairs and through the door.

· 3 ·

I had been in the Cliffside Park Public Library at home a few times. I went on a school trip there every year—they'd show us how to use the library and take us around on a sort of tour. Once I even checked out a couple of books and took them home. It's not that I don't read—I take a few books out of the school library, and I read comics, magazines, and sometimes the newspaper—I just never got around to using the public library much at home. The library at home is nothing like the one in Rochester, which, as I said, is a great big place, and looks like a post office.

I went through the doors into a sort of lobby, then through another doorway into a very large room. The ceiling was made out of little panels of glass, and daylight came through. It was very quiet. "The children's room is upstairs," a lady said to me. I went upstairs. I followed the signs that said CHILDREN'S ROOM.

The children's room was large, with lots of books, nice wood, tables and chairs, and a fireplace. Of course, there wasn't a fire going in it, because it was ninety-six degrees outside according to one of those temperature and time things on a big office building. No one was in the children's room at the time except for a lady sitting at a desk near the entrance. She noticed me coming in. "Did you know that there is a secret door in this room?" she said. "I'm not going to tell you where the secret door is or what is behind it," the lady at the desk said. "But you may look for the secret door and go through it."

I looked at the librarian. She didn't seem to be the sort of person who would play a trick on a kid. I looked around the room. It was a corner room—there were windows on two sides, so there wouldn't be a secret door there—there would be no place for it to lead.

Another wall ran along the hallway—so there would be no secret door there. That left the wall with the fireplace. I'd seen movies on TV where there is a secret door near the fireplace. Usually there is all sorts of fancy carving around the fireplace and the detective, or whoever it is in the movie, pushes a button that looks like part of the carving, and the secret door slides open. But this wasn't that sort of fireplace. There weren't any fancy carvings, just smooth stone. I sort of felt around the fireplace, but I couldn't find anything like a secret door. The other kind of secret door I've seen in movies is the kind where part of the bookshelves swings out on hinges. That made sense in a library. Sure enough, I saw some scratches on the floor in front of a section of bookshelves. When I got closer, I could see two hinges. I took hold of one of the shelves and pulled. The whole section of shelves swung out toward me, and revealed a low door—too low for a grown-up to go through without ducking.

The librarian had gotten up from her desk and come up behind me. "You've found the secret room," she said. "Shall we go in and see what is in it?" She ducked through the door, and I followed her. We entered a small room

17

with a small fireplace that backed up against the big one on the other side of the wall. There were some kid-sized chairs lined up in rows, and a grown-up sized stool off to one side of the fireplace. All around the room were glass cases with lots of dolls—strange ones, all sizes, and in different costumes.

"In the 1930s," the librarian said, "a school here in Rochester had a doll-exchange program with schools all over the world. The children here would send a typical American doll to a school in a foreign country, and the children there would send back a typical doll of their country. Later the whole collection was given to the library."

The dolls were sort of interesting, some of them; about the best ones were two Japanese dolls with all kinds of really lifelike details, elaborate clothing, hairdo, and so forth. I'm not all that interested in dolls, but some of these were very interesting, as I said before.

"We use this secret room as a story room," the librarian went on. "Of course, during the summer, we don't have story hours during the week. Sometimes, during the winter we have a fire in the fireplace."

"Would it be all right for me to come in here?" I asked the librarian. "I mean, if I fries, and a double-thick shake at McTavish's that night. Then he wanted to go for a walk around downtown Rochester. At least it wasn't as hot as it had been earlier in the day. I had been all over the area, so I sort of took the lead and showed Uncle Mel what there was to see. He agreed that the spiral garage was the best thing in town.

"Did you find some things to do?" he wanted to know. I told him that I had spent the afternoon reading in the children's room of the public library. He thought that sounded like a good activity. I told him that it was O.K., but I hoped that I was going to find something else to do before I went through all the books in the place. Uncle Mel said that he would ask some of the guys at the factory if they knew of any interesting things for a kid to do. He also wanted to know if I'd like to come to the factory with him one day and see how everything was made. I wanted to know if I'd be expected to eat any of the slop from the freeze-dried, mix-and-mush micro-wave machine. "Well, you know, we have to be polite," Uncle Mel said. I told him I'd think it over.

We looked in a newspaper and found that a movie about a monster called Yobgorgle that's

wanted to, could I read in this room?"

"I don't see any reason why you shouldn't," the librarian said, "Of course, there aren't any reading tables in this room—but if you think you'd like to read here, please go right ahead."

I don't know why I asked her that. It wasn't such a special room—I mean, after you'd seen the dolls and had the experience of finding the secret door, it was just a room—but it was a secret room, and something about that appealed to me very much. It was just a nice place to be. And it wasn't as bright as the big children's room—the light that came through the window made the room seem as though it was cloudy outside, whereas actually it was blazing hot, and the sun made you squint.

The librarian went back to her desk, and I went out into the big children's room to find something to read. I closed the secret bookshelf door behind me. The librarian had told me to do that so that if any other kid came into the children's room for the first time, they could have the experience of looking for the secret door.

I found a book, an adventure story called *Howard Goldberg, Frontiersman.* It was a story about the first Orthodox Jewish Indian Scout and how he helped to open up the West in the early 1800s. I took the book into the secret room, settled down on the smooth, cool stone floor, and began to read. It was a pretty interesting book. It told about how Howard Goldberg ran away from home in Philadelphia, when he was just a young kid, to go out West and live with the Indians. He showed the Indians how to make bagels out of corn meal, and how to make pastrami from buffalo meat. He hunted bears and raccoons with the Indians, but he wouldn't eat them because they weren't kosher. Years later he met General Custer and told him he was making a big mistake, but nobody listened to him. It was a pretty good book, and it showed how people who belonged to different minorities helped build this country—for example, Howard Goldberg's best friend, who wasn't an Indian, was an Armenian prospector he met in Colorado.

By the time I finished the book, it was pretty late. I heard someone ringing a little bell, like a chime, and saying, "The library will close in fifteen minutes! The library will close in fifteen minutes!" I left the secret room, put my book on the corner of the librarian's desk, the way they told us to on our school trips to the library in Cliffside Park, and went outside.

· 4 ·

I watched TV for a while, had a cola with ice from the ice machine, in one of the plastic glasses from the bathroom, and waited for Uncle Mel to come back. He arrived in a bad mood because he had had to sample all sorts of freeze-dried food from the mix-and-mush micro-wave machines at the factory. "I wouldn't feed that stuff to a cat," Uncle Mel said. "I don't know if I'm going to be able to eat my supper."

It was obvious that Uncle Mel was feeling under the weather, because he only had two Greaso-Whammies, a double order of french

supposed to be real and lives in Lake Ontario was playing at a movie house in a shopping center not too far away. We took a taxi to the shopping center.

The movie was fair. It was a lot like the movie I saw one time about Bigfoot, the monster that's supposed to be real and lives in the North Woods. They had about fifteen seconds of film that might have been a sea monster, or it might have been a big fish or a guy in a monster suit or anything! They showed that fifteen seconds about ten times—regular speed, slow motion, extra slow motion, extra extra slow motion. In between they showed various people who claimed to have seen Yobgorgle, and they showed drawings that people who had supposedly seen Yobgorgle had made. Too bad none of the people who had seen Yobgorgle knew how to draw—all the drawings looked like a first-grader had done them, and all of them were different.

Then they showed professors in various laboratories talking about whether they thought Yobgorgle might really exist. There was this real heavy narration all through the movie: "DOES YOBGORGLE EXIST? THIS MARINE BIOLOGIST, EQUIPPED WITH ALL THE MOST

MODERN SCIENTIFIC DEVICES THINKS HE WILL FIND HIM." Then the movie showed this weirdo in a big rowboat with all kinds of ropes and nets and a thing for listening to fish, floating around in the lake.

Then the weirdo in the boat turned around to the camera, and took the pipe out of his mouth. The narrator said, "THIS MAN IS PROFESSOR AMBROSE McFWAIN OF THE PISCEAN DISCOVERY INSTITUTE IN ROCHESTER, NEW YORK. PROFESSOR McFWAIN TELLS OF HIS EXPERIENCES IN TRACKING THIS STRANGE MONSTER."

Professor Ambrose McFwain scratched his beard with the end of his pipe. "I think I may have actually heard Yobgorgle. One night I was rowing my research vessel in the vicinity of Irondequoit Bay. I had my earphones on, and the tape recorder attached to my supersonic listening device. I was recording the usual sounds of Lake Ontario on a summer evening. Then I heard something quite unusual. At first it sounded very much like a 1956 Chevy with bad valves that I used to own. Of course, there would be no way for a 1956 Chevy to be that far out in the lake.

"The sound was very clear and sounded as though it was near my boat. I took off my earphones and found that I could hear the sound much better. I was trolling a hydrophone—that's an underwater microphone—at fifteen feet, but this sound was coming from the surface! It was a very dark night. I couldn't see anything very clearly, but I thought I saw something dark on the surface of the water about fifty yards away. It sounded like a '56 Chevy, as I said, or a monster breathing. Those are the only two things it could have been. I reached for my special waterproof camera with infrared flash, but just as I got the thing up to my eye, I heard a splash, and the dark thing on the surface of the water disappeared. At the same moment, I flashed my picture. When it was developed, this is what I saw."

Professor Ambrose McFwain, of the Piscean Discovery Institute held up a snapshot—you couldn't make out anything but glare from the movie lights.

"As you can see," Professor Ambrose Mc-Fwain said, "the picture at first appears to be nothing but bubbles and lake mist, but if you look closely, you will see a faint red light—right here." He pointed with his pipe. "This could only be the tail light of a '56 Chevy or the eye of a monster. There is no explanation as to what a

'56 Chevy would be doing that far out in the lake. So I believe the only reasonable explanation is that I had encountered some strange life-form in the lake. I believe that what I heard and almost saw and very nearly photographed that night was Yobgorgle."

Then the movie showed the fifteen seconds of film for the tenth time. Then it showed all of the people who had talked about their Yobgorgle experiences, and the drawings, and the shots of newspaper headlines, and the professors in their laboratories, and Ambrose McFwain in his rowboat, and the narrator said, "YOBGORGLE! IS IT A FOLKTALE OR IS IT A REALITY? WE HAVE SHOWN YOU THE FACTS—THE DECISION IS UP TO YOU."

Then the movie was over. Even with repeating everything four or five times, it still only ran a little over an hour and a half. Then there were four cartoons—old ones—and a short subject about boating in Australia, and the house lights came on.

Uncle Mel spent some time looking at the food vending machines in the lobby of the movie house while we waited for the taxi he had called to come and pick us up.

We got to McTavish's just before closing

time. The movie apparently helped Uncle Mel get his appetite back because he got into some heavy cheeseburger eating. They were mopping up McTavish's when we left. We walked back to the motel.

Before going to sleep, we watched a talk show on television. One of the advertisements they ran in between was for the movie we'd just seen. The ad was a lot better than the movie—it had all the good stuff in the movie in it. Also the ad only took about thirty seconds, while the movie was about one hundred and eighty times as long, and didn't contain any more information.

· 5 ·

The next morning, after eating my egg McTavish with Uncle Mel, I headed straight for the library. The day was going to be another scorcher, and I didn't feel like doing any exploring. I wanted to get inside the cool library as soon as possible.

The lady was sitting at the desk. She said hello to me. I asked her if she had any books about Yobgorgle. She didn't know what Yobgorgle was—I guess she didn't watch much television or go to the movies. I told her that Yobgorgle was a monster that lived in Lake Ontario.

28

The librarian said that she might have a book on sea monsters. I went with her, and together we looked it up in the card catalog.

"Here it is," she said. *"Great Sea Monsters I Have Known* by Professor Ambrose McFwain of the Piscean Discovery Institute, right here in Rochester."

It was by the same guy—the weird guy in the boat—the one with the beard that I had seen in the movie the night before! I took the book and went into the secret room to read it. It was a pretty interesting book, but Professor Ambrose McFwain didn't really give any proof for the things he said in it. He talked about the Loch Ness monster. He said he had seen it clear as you like, but when he tried to take its picture, he forgot and left the lens cap on his camera. Another monster he wrote about was Moby Dick, the great white whale. He said that Moby Dick was real and that Herman Melville, who wrote the story about him, had seen him, but he didn't give any proof of that either. Then he went on to write about a monster called Ogo Pogo—no proof—and about his expedition to find Tieholtsodi. Tieholtsodi was a sea monster mentioned in Navajo Indian myths. According to the myths, Tieholtsodi lived in the Eastern Water.

Professor Ambrose McFwain figured out that the Navajos, when they said Eastern Water, meant Lake Michigan. So he went to Chicago and started asking people if they had ever heard anything about a monster living in the lake. He didn't get anywhere, but in Evanston, Illinois, he found a bunch of people who said they had seen a monster. They called it Knob Ears. Ambrose McFwain decided that this must be the same Tieholtsodi mentioned in the Navajo myths.

He hired a boat and a guide named Reynold, who claimed to have seen Knob Ears a number of times. They spent several days floating around Lake Michigan before dawn, looking for Knob Ears. This time Professor McFwain did find the monster and actually got his pictures.

But on the way home, Reynold, the guide, went crazy in the boat. He took off his shoes and stood up and started to dance around and mutter all sorts of strange things. As a result, the boat was swamped, the camera and film were lost, and Professor McFwain and Reynold arrived back at the dock very wet.

It seemed to me that Professor Ambrose McFwain had very little luck in his sea-monster tracking. But he kept at it. He was determined.

He said that the one greatest deed of his career would be finding Yobgorgle. He had moved to Rochester, New York, to be near Lake Ontario, and started the Piscean Discovery Institute, which was supposed to encourage all sincere sea-monster finders everywhere, but was primarily for the purpose of finding Yobgorgle.

I don't know if any of this would have been as interesting to me if I had read about it back home in Cliffside Park, but here in Rochester where the search for Yobgorgle was actually going on, after seeing the not-very-good movie about Yobgorgle, and then finding the book by Professor McFwain—I was getting sort of interested in the whole project. It hadn't taken long to read the book by Professor McFwain. There were lots of pictures—old ones of what people imagined sea monsters looked like—and there was very large type and a lot of white space. I looked at the clock in the big children's room when I had finished the book. It was only ten-thirty. I still had the whole day ahead of me. I really didn't feel like reading another book right away, so I put my copy of *Great Sea Monsters I Have Known* on the corner of the librarian's desk and went downstairs.

I stood for a while in the lobby of the library.

It was too early to go to Bob's Beanery for lunch. The egg McTavish still lay in my stomach, like an undissolved glob of plastic. I didn't feel bored now so much as anxious. I wanted to do something, but I didn't know quite what it was. In the lobby of the library there was a telephone booth. Outside it on a slanting shelf was a telephone book. I looked up the Piscean Discovery Institute.

"See McFwain Foundation," read the telephone book.

I looked up the McFwain Foundation. "See McFwain Institute," it said in the telephone book.

I looked up the McFwain Institute. "See Professor Ambrose McFwain," it said.

I looked up Professor Ambrose McFwain. "See McFwain Toy Company," the book said.

I looked up the McFwain Toy Company. There was a telephone number. I went into the phone booth, dropped in a dime, and dialed the number.

The dime clicked. The number rang. Some one answered.

"Hello. E. J. Kupeckzky Thought Factory," the voice on the telephone said.

"Excuse me," I said. "I was calling the McFwain Toy Company."

"This is the McFwain Toy Company," the voice said.

"Oh—well, actually," I said, "I was calling the Piscean Discovery Institute."

"This is also the Piscean Discovery Institute," said the voice.

"Uh—I was wondering—I wanted to talk to Professor McFwain."

"You *are* talking to Professor McFwain. What can I do for you?"

I didn't really know what Professor Ambrose McFwain could do for me. I guessed he was a very busy man, what with the Piscean Discovery Institute, the McFwain Foundation, the McFwain Institute, the McFwain Toy Company, and the E. J. Kupeckzky Thought Factory to run. I didn't know what to say to him. For a second I thought of just hanging up, but that would have been too rude. "Uh—I was—uh—I read your book. . . ."

"Which one?"

"I read *Great Sea Monsters I Have Known*, and I saw that movie you're in. . . ."

"How'd you like the movie?"

"Well, uh, not too much. I thought it was pretty long and it just kept repeating the same information over and over again."

"Are you a fellow scientist?"

"Well, actually, I'm just a. . . ."

"Of course, you are," said Professor Ambrose McFwain. "Tell you what—I'd love to talk over scientific matters with you, but I'm just going to duck out for a bite. Why don't you join me for lunch? You know where the downtown branch of McTavish's is, don't you?"

"I had breakfast there," I said.

"I hope you don't mind eating there twice in one day," Professor Ambrose McFwain said.

"I expected to eat there twice today," I said.

"Good for you! You know what you like, and you stick with it. I'll meet you there in fifteen minutes." Then Professor Ambrose McFwain hung up.

· 6 ·

I arrived at McTavish's in less than fifteen minutes. I went to the counter, got a Greaso-Junior and a thick shake, and sat down where I could see the door. I wondered why Professor Ambrose McFwain wanted to have lunch with me. Maybe he didn't realize that I was a kid. Maybe he just thought I was someone with a high voice. Maybe he thought I was a lady. That would be embarrassing. Maybe he thought he was going to have lunch with a lady. Sometimes people call up at home to try and sell my mother encyclopedias or home delivery of the newspaper, and they think I'm her. Uncle Mel says my voice will change later. I hope it doesn't change to a voice like his—it's higher than mine and sort of squeaky—no, whistley. Uncle Mel's voice sounds like a boat whistle.

I was thinking about all this stuff when Professor Ambrose McFwain came in. He looked just the way he had in the movie. I got up. "Excuse me, Professor McFwain," I said.

"Ah, you're the young man I'm supposed to have lunch with," Professor McFwain said. "I see you've gotten your food already—good idea, avoid the lunch rush—that's why I come here no later than eleven o'clock. I'll just get a few things and join you. I won't be a minute."

Professor Ambrose McFwain was back in a little while with a tray piled high with everything McTavish's sells. "This guy would get along fine with my Uncle Mel," I thought.

"I'm Eugene Winkleman," I said.

"Delighted," Professor Ambrose McFwain said, and dived into his tray of paper and plastic-wrapped junk food. While he ate, every now and then he'd say, "Mmmmmmm," or "Aaaah!" or "Superb!"

When Professor McFwain had finished packing away a meal that would have been worthy of Uncle Mel, he rolled all the napkins and

paper and plastic wrappers into a big ball between his palms. "Now," he said, "let's get
down to business. I'll come straight to the point
and tell you that there are no other candidates,
and you've got the job as my assistant for two
weeks, beginning tomorrow."

"The job as your assistant?" I was a little be-
wildered, but when he said it, I realized that
somehow or other that *was* the sort of thing I
had in mind.

"Yes, don't you want to help me find Yobgorgle?" Professor McFwain said, "It's been
two weeks since I ran the newspaper ad for a
volunteer to help me—and frankly, you're the
first applicant."

"I'll have to ask Uncle Mel," I said.

"Who's Uncle Mel?"

"My uncle."

"Well, let's ask him."

Professor Ambrose McFwain gave me a card
with the address of the McFwain Toy Company
on it. "Just drop by at seven o'clock," he said.
"If that's convenient for your uncle. We'll talk it
over then." He looked at his watch. "Well, well,
I've got to run. I've got an order for six thousand
Yobgorgle dolls to get out."

"You sell Yobgorgle dolls?" I asked.

"Hottest new toy of the year," Professor Ambrose McFwain said.

"But nobody has ever seen Yobgorgle," I said.

"That's not true," Professor McFwain said. "Lots of people have seen Yobgorgle. It's just that nobody reliable has ever seen it. You and I are going to be the first reputable scientists to see it."

"I'm not a reputable scientist. I'm only a kid," I said.

"Never say that!" Professor McFwain said. "Mozart wrote great music when he was three. Thomas Edison invented all sorts of things when he was only a boy. And I myself invented the dill pickle when I was six years old. You never know what you can do until you try."

"You are the inventor of the dill pickle?" I asked.

"I have that honor," Professor Ambrose McFwain said.

"Wow!" I said.

"I thought you'd be impressed," Professor McFwain said. "I'll see you at seven tonight."

Professor Ambrose McFwain hurried out of McTavish's, still rolling the ball of wrappers and napkins between his palms. He was obviously as crazy as a loon, but I liked him. He didn't make anything special of my being a kid—I mean, he treated me like a regular person.

I still had quite a bit of time until Uncle Mel came back to the motel. I decided that if I was going to be a scientist's assistant, I might as well do some extra reading, sort of research to prepare for my job.

I used the big card catalog downstairs in the adult department. I found three books by Professor Ambrose McFwain, *How I Invented the Dill Pickle—and How the Idea Was Stolen from Me; My Expedition to the Lost Civilization of Waka-Waka;* and *The Research Scientist and Monster-Hunter's Handbook.*

The first two books were out, the librarian in the adult department told me, but they had *The Research Scientist and Monster-Hunter's Handbook.* I asked the librarian in the adult department if I could take the book upstairs and read it in the children's room. She said it would be all right.

I took the book upstairs into the secret room. One nice thing about Professor Ambrose Mc-Fwain's books—they were easy to read. This one had big print, lots of white space, and lots of pictures. The book was full of advice for monster-hunters and researchers. It started with a chapter about photography:

PHOTOGRAPHING MONSTERS

It is a good idea to take pictures of the various monsters you will be tracking. Any sort of camera will do, but certain rules should be observed. First, take film along. There is nothing as frustrating as coming upon a monster, hitherto unknown to science, in some uncharted place like the Arctic tundra, the Amazon River basin, or the Gobi Desert, only to discover that you don't have any film. The author has learned this "trick of the trade" from painful experience in all those places.

Next, the best camera in the world will not take a suitable picture if you forget to take the lens cap off. Learn from the tragic experience of this author—take off that lens cap!

Another thing which can go wrong with photographing monsters is to accidentally let your thumb or finger or beard get in the way of the lens when taking the picture. This, too, has happened to the author in the heat of the chase.

There is a lot that can go wrong with photographic equipment. Lack of film, leaving the lens cap on, getting one's thumb or beard in front of the lens—this will explain to the reader why there are so few pictures of monsters available.

The book went on with good advice like that for scientists and monster-hunters. There was a long chapter on what kind of shoes to wear when going after monsters (loose); what kind of bags to put your lunch in (waterproof); how to approach a monster in the wild (with caution). It was a very informative book. I liked it better than Professor McFwain's other book because it got right to the point and gave helpful suggestions. After reading it, I felt that I was really ready to help Professor McFwain look for the monster Yobgorgle.

When Uncle Mel got back to the motel that night, he was really bugged. "Guess what they made me eat from that horrible machine," he said. I couldn't guess. "Salad!" he said. "Freeze-dried, reconstituted, mixed-and-mushed chef's salad! With Italian dressing! I thought I was going to die!"

"Did it taste like salad?" I asked.

"It tasted exactly like salad!" he said. "I hate salad!"

"I wonder how they do the lettuce," I said.

"It's an engineering miracle," Uncle Mel said.

"Look," I said, "I've been offered a part-time job, and I want to take it. It only lasts two weeks, so I could do it while we're here."

"A job? What sort of job?" Uncle Mel asked.

"It's helping a scientist—I think he may be a mad scientist—look for a sea monster that lives in Lake Ontario."

"It sounds educational," Uncle Mel said, "I guess your parents would approve."

"He wants us to come to his office at seven o'clock," I said. "He gave me a card with his address."

"O.K.," Uncle Mel said. "After supper. I really need a few Greaso-Whammies to get the taste of that salad out of my mouth."

· 7 ·

Professor McFwain's office was in the basement of a building on North Water Street, right near the river. Uncle Mel asked the desk clerk at the motel how to get there, and we walked. It was just a couple of blocks from McTavish's. The rest of the building was a factory where they make clothes for fat guys. Uncle Mel, who must weigh two hundred and eighty pounds was glad to know about the factory. He said he might come back and get a suit.

There was a little sign near the steps to the basement door. It said McFWAIN TOY COM-PANY, INC., and there was an arrow pointing

43

down the stairs. At the bottom of the stairs were all kinds of waste paper and garbage that had blown down there. There was a metal door, painted gray with big round rivets in it, and a doorbell button. Uncle Mel pushed the button.

"Just a minute! I'm coming." I could hear Professor McFwain's voice from somewhere inside the building.

The door opened. There was Professor McFwain. He was wearing a fancy bathrobe with a dragon embroidered on the pocket. When he turned to lead us into the building, we could see that there was also a dragon embroidered on the back. The bathrobe was about five sizes too big for Professor McFwain. I guess it had been made in the fat guys' clothing factory upstairs.

"Welcome to my toy company, my research facility and my humble home," Professor McFwain said. "You see, I have a very economical arrangement with the company that owns this building. In return for my services as night watchman, I get the use of my basement apartment and offices free. I also get a fabulous discount on clothes. Unfortunately, size 50 is the smallest they make."

He took off the dragon bathrobe. Underneath

it he was wearing the same suit I had seen him in earlier that day. "You must be Uncle Mel," Professor McFwain said. "Here, try this on. I think it may fit you."

Uncle Mel tried on the bathrobe. He was obviously delighted with it.

"Please take it as a present," Professor Mc-Fwain said. "It didn't cost me a penny—it's a sample they made up and decided not to manufacture. I have a friend in the design department who lets me have things like this. It's brand-new. If you don't like the color, there are five or six others upstairs."

"No, bright red is fine," Uncle Mel said, "I've always wanted a bathrobe like this."

"I'm delighted to have met someone who's . . . uh . . . substantial enough to wear it," Professor McFwain said. "Now, here we are at my quarters."

All this time Professor Ambrose McFwain had been leading us through all sorts of dimly lit corridors, storerooms, boiler rooms, and similar stuff that you find in basements. He opened a door on which there was a sign reading McFWAIN TOY CO. We entered a large room with a big wooden table in the middle and shelves along the walls. On the shelves were green plastic dolls looking a little like a dragon with a bushy beard and three eyes.

"These are the Yobgorgle dolls," Professor McFwain said. "I'm making a fortune selling them. I have them made up in a factory in Iceland, and they're shipped here, and I distribute them. There's such a demand for them that I've shipped every one I've got, except these few that I keep for samples. I'm presently waiting for more. They'll be arriving from Iceland in about two weeks, which gives me some time to go out looking for the real Yobgorgle. That's where young Eugene comes in. I need a bright young fellow to go along with me, help with the research, and handle the boat while I take a few pictures. It's an opportunity not many young boys get."

"Now I know who you are!" Uncle Mel said. "You were in that movie we saw last night! You were the guy in the boat!"

"Quite right," Professor Ambrose McFwain said. "Now, if you'll excuse me, I think I hear the doorbell. I took the liberty of calling out for five double-giant pizzas with everything. I thought we might munch while we talk. I'll go answer the door. You'll find some gallon bottles of root beer in that little refrigerator; and if you don't mind, please put some ice in those glasses. I'll be right back."

When Professor McFwain had gone, Uncle Mel said, "He seems to be a really fine man, Eugene. I think you can learn a lot working as his assistant."

Naturally, Uncle Mel and Professor McFwain hit it off beautifully. Two born eaters and guzzlers, they ate four and a half double-giant pizzas with everything while they talked, and consumed a gallon and three-quarters of root beer. Professor McFwain wanted to hear all about the freeze-dried, micro-wave, mix-and-mush machine; and Uncle Mel wanted to hear all about Professor McFwain's toy business, the stories (all of which I had read in his book) about his career as a monster-hunter, and different junk food places in Rochester.

While they talked, I looked at maps of the shoreline of Lake Ontario, which Professor McFwain had marked with *X*'s to show places where Yobgorgle had been sighted.

"About this monster-hunting," Uncle Mel asked. "I don't suppose there's any danger? I wouldn't want Eugene's parents to get mad at me—not that I expect anything will happen to him."

"Danger?" said Professor McFwain. "Danger? Sir, monster-hunting is the most dangerous occupation there is—there's no use denying it. Of course, with me, the boy will be as safe as anyone could be when tracking something which, I believe, will turn out to be better than a hundred yards long, and goodness knows how wild. By the way, you haven't got any use for a fancy cowboy suit, have you? They have one upstairs that was made for a famous country and western singer, but he went on a diet and they never delivered it."

"What sort of a cowboy suit is it?" Uncle Mel asked.

"Oh, it's terrific!" Ambrose McFwain said. "It has all sorts of fancy Indian embroidery, and a hat that goes with it, and everything. I could ask my friend if they want to get rid of it."

"Well, I have sort of always wanted a cowboy suit," Uncle Mel said. "Nothing too loud, you understand, just something I could wear to a party."

"This one will be perfect for you," Professor McFwain said. "And about that other matter—don't worry."

"Don't worry?"

"Don't worry."

"Well, Professor, I feel sure that Eugene will

have a really valuable educational experience working with you," Uncle Mel said. "And if they feel they don't need the cowboy suit. . . ."

"I'll send it along with Eugene," Professor McFwain said.

I had been worried for a while that Uncle Mel might decide that monster-hunting was too dangerous an occupation for a kid and not give me permission to go. But he liked Professor McFwain too much—and apparently he wanted that cowboy suit. Ordinarily, Uncle Mel just wore these rumpled-looking gray suits. I never knew he was interested in clothes. Maybe it's hard for fat guys to get nice clothes.

Back in the motel room, Uncle Mel spent a lot of time looking at himself in the mirror, wearing the dragon bathrobe. Then he went out to an all-night drugstore and came back with a pipe. Then he spent a lot of time looking at himself in the mirror, wearing the dragon bathrobe and smoking the pipe. It stank up the room.

Professor McFwain had told me to turn up at his office early the next morning, so I went to bed. Uncle Mel was watching a late movie, and before I fell asleep I saw him get up every now and then and look at himself in his new pipe and bathrobe.

· 8 ·

As soon as I had eaten my egg McTavish with Uncle Mel, I hurried right over to North Water Street to report to Professor Ambrose McFwain. When I arrived, the fat men's clothing factory was in full operation. I could hear different kinds of machinery, sewing machines and other stuff, all the way down the block. Trucks were pulled up to the loading dock, and fat employees were loading boxes on some trucks and unloading bolts of cloth from others, while fat truck drivers stood around drinking soda pop and telling jokes. It was a busy place.

I went down the basement stairs, and through

the gray metal door—it was open. The basement of the fat men's clothing factory was cool and dim. I got a little lost, but finally I found Professor McFwain's office. He was sitting at the big conference table, eating a hero sandwich wrapped in cellophane.

"Ah! Eugene!" Professor McFwain said. "Are you ready to begin your exciting new career as a monster-hunter?"

"I certainly am, Professor," I said. "Are we going out after Yobgorgle right now?"

"Ah, the enthusiasm of the young!" Professor McFwain said. "There it is—in a nutshell—youth versus experience. Monster-hunting, like most other things, is ninety-eight percent preparation plus one percent action and one percent luck. I'm afraid that monster-hunting is not all glamor and flash like you've seen in the movies."

If he was thinking about the movie I'd seen about Yobgorgle with Uncle Mel the other night, it showed monster-hunting as one hundred percent talk, with no action and no luck.

"You see," Professor McFwain went on, "any fool can go out in the lake and just run into Yobgorgle by dumb luck. In fact, that's how

51

every sighting of Yobgorgle so far has happened. Some ordinary citizen is out fishing or sailing for pleasure, and, bang, there's the monster. He gets scared, doesn't observe closely, tells his story in a disorganized fashion—and what do you have? Inconclusive data! But we are scientists. We have to prepare, prepare, prepare! When we find the monster, it won't come as a surprise. We'll be ready to take his picture, measure him, shake hands—or shake fins—with him, and say 'how do you do.' That's what we want. So we have to make sure that we are ready mentally, physically, and scientifically. Today, we are going to begin to assemble needed equipment."

Professor McFwain took another bite of his sandwich. "What we are going to do today, Eugene, is acquire a field research vehicle, which will serve as our traveling laboratory. It will allow us to transport the McFwain Institute research vessel from place to place, act as a portable photographic darkroom, and also enable us to go to drive-in restaurants in the suburbs. I have just such a machine in mind, and I've been waiting almost a year to buy it. And today is the only day in the year to do so."

"Why is that?" I asked Professor McFwain

"Do you believe in astrology, or something like that?"

"Certainly not!" he said. "I am a scientist. The reason that this is the only day in the year to buy our research vehicle, or any sort of a car or truck, is that this is the only day in the year when Colonel Ken Krenwinkle sells cars."

"Who is Colonel Ken Krenwinkle?" I asked.

"Colonel Ken Krenwinkle is the richest man in Rochester. He may be the richest man in the United States or the richest man in the world—nobody knows how rich he is. To give you an idea of how rich he is, he once bought the entire State of Florida, because he liked an amusement park there. But later he got tired of it, and sold the whole state to real estate developers."

The Professor threw his sandwich wrapper in the wastebasket and unwrapped a big slice of cake. "What Colonel Ken Krenwinkle likes to do best is sell cars. He used to get in trouble by going to used car lots on Sundays, when they were closed, and pretending to be a salesman. He'd make all sorts of deals with people who came to look at the cars—selling them for a dollar or offering to give the people money to take the cars away—and he'd write up the deals on little slips of paper. Then on Monday morning, when the real used car dealer came to open his business, there would be lines of people thinking that they'd bought cars at bargain prices, waiting to pick up their purchases. Colonel Ken Krenwinkle was always getting sued by used car dealers."

Professor McFwain offered me a piece of the cake. I took it gladly. Then he continued: "Of course, the Colonel could buy his own used car lot, but he never did that. Maybe it came of being disappointed when he bought the State of Florida and then got tired of it. What Colonel Ken Krenwinkle does now, is buy a different used car lot every year on the same day—that is, he buys every car on the lot and then spends a day making deals. Quite a few people know about Colonel Ken Krenwinkle's strange hobby and take advantage of the unusual deals he makes. But they never know which used car lot he has bought—and since he appears in a disguise every year, there is no sure way to find out if he's really the one selling the cars on a given lot. Of course, the other used car dealers know which day of the year Colonel Ken Krenwinkle does his car-selling, so they all put on fake beards and dark glasses on that day and trot out all the old junkers they haven't been able to sell all year, and offer them at bargain prices. No one is ever sure if they're buying a fantastic bargain from Colonel Ken Krenwinkle or a cheap, but worthless, rusted-out hulk from a regular used car dealer. It's very exciting."

"And this is the day?"

"This is the day. What's more, I have pretty good information about which used car lot has been bought up by the real Colonel Ken Krenwinkle. And, as luck would have it, on that used car lot is the perfect research field vehicle for my purposes, a four-wheel drive, Hindustan-eight—a fine machine of Indian make, not seen very often in this country. So without further ado, let's go and see if we can buy it for a very low price."

"What kind of unusual deals does Colonel Ken Krenwinkle make?" I asked.

"Well, it varies from year to year," Professor McFwain said. "For example, once he sold a nearly brand-new, last year's model car, super deluxe, with air conditioning, stereo, whitewall tires, and all sorts of extras for $27.95. The unusual part of the deal was that the car came with, as an extra that you were required to buy, a stuffed gorilla tied to the roof with rope. The

55

gorilla cost $12.00 extra. And the buyer had to sign a contract saying that he would leave the stuffed gorilla where it was. If he removed the gorilla, and Colonel Ken Krenwinkle found out about it, then the buyer would have to give back the car. Someone bought it, and you can see it sometimes around town with the stuffed gorilla tied to the roof. That is the sort of unusual deal Colonel Ken Krenwinkle makes.

"Another time, Colonel Ken Krenwinkle sold a car—and the buyer had to sign a paper promising to paint his house blue—Colonel Ken Krenwinkle supplied the paint. Another time, he sold a car with a huge sign on top saying DON'T EAT DUCKS! The buyer had to promise to leave the sign. But why are we sitting around here talking? Let's get going before the Hindustan is sold!"

Professor McFwain and I went outside and caught a bus. We got off in front of a used car lot, which had a big sign saying

RIDICULOUS ROOSMAN
THE SENTIMENTAL SRI LANKESE—
EVERY VEHICLE,
A TRANSPORT OF DELIGHT.

· 9 ·

In the middle of the used car lot stood a man wearing a heavy winter overcoat, blue sunglasses, and a beard that was obviously a fake. When we got closer, it was apparent that his nose was made out of putty.

"Is that Colonel Ken Krenwinkle?" I whispered to Professor Ambrose McFwain.

"I believe it is," he whispered back. "But we'll only know for sure when he closes the deal. Just act natural and don't say anything."

"Ah, gentlemen," the man in the heavy overcoat, blue sunglasses, fake beard and putty nose said. "May I help you this beautiful morning?"

"Are you the proprietor?" Professor Ambrose McFwain asked.

"I am he. I am Ridiculous Roosman, the Sentimental Sri Lankese, from Sri Lanka, which used to be called Ceylon. My father and my father's father were dealers in fine used elephants. I have come here and sell the finest of second-hand cars in my beloved adopted country, sirs."

Ridiculous Roosman, the sentimental Sri Lankese, if that was really who he was, didn't sound like he came from Ceylon. Not that I know what a Ceylonese or a Sri Lankese is supposed to sound like, but this man had a regular American Southern accent, like someone from Georgia or Alabama.

"I noticed that Hindustan-eight panel truck," Professor Ambrose McFwain said. "Not to waste your time, I'm not really interested in buying it, but I thought it would be amusing if you'd show it to me and my young friend here."

"Think nothing of it," said Ridiculous Roosman. "I am here exclusively for your pleasure. If you wish to buy a fine car, naturally, that will make me the happiest man on earth—but if you would enjoy just looking, or throwing cold spaghetti in my face, or knocking me down and

58

stamping on me—in fact, anything which would give you a moment's fleeting pleasure would bring me ultimate joy. You wish to see the Hindustan-eight. You shall see it. You may feel free to inspect it as minutely as you like. Kick it, hammer on it, set fire to it. Your slightest wish is my command."

While he was talking, Ridiculous Roosman was leading us to a little green truck with rusty bumpers. "This is a fine and, if I may say so, a very rare vehicle," the sentimental Sri Lankese said. "Needless to say, it is in perfect running order—just listen to this. . . ."

Ridiculous Roosman reached inside the Hindustan-eight and pulled a wooden handle, which had a long cord attached to it, like the thing they use to start outboard motors. The cord was wound around a metal spool, which spun when he pulled the handle, and the motor began to cough and sputter. Clouds of black smoke poured out of the tailpipe and from under the hood.

"A masterpiece of engineering," the sentimental Sri Lankese said.

Professor McFwain walked around the truck, kicking the tires, and grabbing at the fenders, which made a soft crunching noise when he rocked them back and forth and showered little reddish flakes of rust on the ground. "It seems to have had a bit of use," Professor McFwain said.

"No, that's the way they're built. This car will never rust any more than it has rusted already. They come from the factory pre-rusted."

"Oh, I didn't know that," Professor McFwain said. "How much are you asking for this machine?"

"Well, this is actually a collector's item," Ridiculous Roosman said. "There are only two or three of them in this country. I could sell this over the telephone to a collector in Oswego for $20,000, but because I like you very much, if you wish, it's yours for $19,500."

Professor McFwain made a face.

"Or," Ridiculous Roosman continued, "I could make the price a little lower, if you are interested in a special deal."

"Here it comes," Professor McFwain whispered to me.

"In the event that you will agree to certain conditions by which I can advertise my business, I will make a substantial reduction in the price."

"How much of a reduction?" Professor McFwain said.

"I'll sell you the automobile for $3.00, but there is a condition," the car dealer said.

"I accept your offer, Colonel Ken Krenwinkle," Professor McFwain said.

"Colonel? Colonel? I am no Colonel. In the Sri Lanka Jiujitsu Self-Defense Forces, I was only a private. I don't know what you're talking about."

"Excuse me," Professor McFwain said. "For a moment, I thought you were someone else. Now, what was the condition?"

"Now we're getting someplace," said Ridiculous Roosman. "You may purchase this magnificent Hindustan-eight motor vehicle for the full price of $3.00, if you will sign a legally binding agreement to wear this costume whenever you drive it."

Ridiculous Roosman reached into the back of the little green truck and brought out a big white feathery thing. "If you will agree to wear this chicken suit whenever you drive it, the machine is yours for $3.00. Try it on—let's see how you look in it."

Professor McFwain climbed into the chicken suit. "It's sort of comfortable, actually," he said. "I'll agree to the deal."

"Bravo!" Ridiculous Roosman said. "I knew you were a sport the minute I saw you. I'll get the papers for you to sign."

"Are you really going to drive around wearing that chicken suit?" I asked the Professor.

"It's not so bad," the Professor said, "the beak makes a sort of visor. It will keep the sun out of my eyes. Besides, it's not what you wear that's the important thing. It's who you are—inside."

The sentimental Sri Lankese came back with the papers for Professor Ambrose McFwain to sign. When the Professor had signed his name, the used car dealer got very excited. "Professor Ambrose McFwain! The very man I've been wanting to meet! You are the man who is going to find Yobgorgle, are you not?"

"That is my mission," Professor McFwain said, as he handed over the $3.00. "Allow me to introduce Eugene Winkleman, my young assistant. Now, since we've concluded our deal, wouldn't you like to reveal your true identity?"

"Yes, of course. It's an honor to meet you, sir," said the used car salesman, pulling off his fake beard. "I am, as you have already guessed, Colonel Ken Krenwinkle, at your service." He shook hands with both of us. "You know, I truly admire the work you are doing. I'd be proud to offer you any help in my power, and also I'd like very much to go out looking for the monster with you."

"And so you shall!" Professor Ambrose McFwain said. "We will be proud to have you join our expedition."

"Oh, thank you," Colonel Ken Krenwinkle said. "Here is my card. I can always be reached through this telephone number."

"I'll be in touch with you within the week, never fear," Professor McFwain said.

The two men shook hands, Professor Mc-Fwain pulled down the visor of his chicken suit, and we both climbed into the Hindustan-eight. The Professor yanked the wooden handle to start the motor, put it into gear, and we rattled out into the street.

· 10 ·

We were rumbling and rattling through the midday traffic. The Hindustan-eight was trailing black, oily smoke. "This is a truly magnificent machine," Professor McFwain said.

"It seems sort of crummy and beat-up to me," I said.

"That's only because you are not familiar with its unique design," Professor McFwain said. "This machine doesn't operate on conventional automotive principles; instead it is built along the lines of obscure Vedic philosophies of India. It's too complicated to understand unless you are well-versed in the wisdom of the

East—but suffice it to say, this is the ideal car, the *only* car to have a real adventure in. And how about that Colonel Ken Krenwinkle? Isn't he a fine man? And a philanthropist—why he practically gave us the car. What a selfless contribution to science!"

"He made you wear the chicken suit," I said.

"You know, I rather like this chicken suit," Professor McFwain said. "You'd think it would be warm, but I get a nice breeze through the feathers."

"Professor McFwain," I said, "a lot of people are staring at us."

"You've got to expect that when you drive a classic car," he said. "Now, I'm famished after all that haggling. What say we motor out to Braddock Point and have a look for Yobgorgle or any signs thereof, and on the way we can stop at Fred's Fat Pig, a really superior drive-in restaurant. They have a six level super cheeseburger that is fit for a king."

Professor McFwain stepped on the accelerator, and the Hindustan-eight sort of threw itself forward—the car had a desperate way of moving, as though it were hurling itself off a cliff.

Professor McFwain evidently enjoyed driving, even though the car shuddered as though it was terrified, lurched, hesitated, and then lurched forward again. I wasn't sure if it was the Hindustan-eight or the way Professor McFwain drove—maybe a little of each.

As he drove, Professor Ambrose McFwain talked and chattered continuously. "Well, well, our expedition is taking shape, is it not? Now Colonel Ken Krenwinkle wants to join us—I trust him, don't you? I'll wager he's a good man in a tight place—military background—must have gotten that title somewhere. He's our man in case of a crisis. What about your uncle Mel? Do you think he'd like to join us? There can't be much to interest a man of his obvious taste and culture in Rochester of a weekend—maybe he'd like to come aboard on a part-time basis, when he's not engaged in his business activities."

I told Professor McFwain that I'd ask Uncle Mel if he would like to come along and look for Yobgorgle, and I reminded Professor McFwain about the cowboy suit, as Uncle Mel had asked me to.

"Oh, yes, the cowboy suit! That's all arranged. The factory says he can have it. If we get back this afternoon before my friend goes home, I'll send it along with you this very evening."

We arrived at Fred's Fat Pig. We pulled up outside and Professor McFwain honked the horn. It was the first time I'd ever seen one of those horns that you honk by squeezing a rubber bulb. A waitress wearing a pig mask came out and gave us menus. When she walked away, I noticed that there was a curly pig's tail attached to the back of her uniform.

"This is a high-class place," Professor McFwain said.

The waitress in the pig mask and tail didn't seem to take any notice of the fact that the man she was serving was dressed in a chicken suit. I guess that people who are dressed up as animals start to take it for granted after a while.

We ate right in the car. The waitress fastened little metal trays to the windows, and we ate from them. As I ate my six-level cheeseburger, the thought crossed my mind that it would be more than a month before my mother got home and gave me some real food. I wondered how long a human being could survive on the stuff that Uncle Mel and Professor McFwain ate. They were alive, of course, but Uncle Mel was fat and Professor McFwain was crazy. I wondered if a steady diet of fast food had done that to them.

After our meal, Professor McFwain started up the Hindustan-eight, and we headed for Braddock Point on the shore of Lake Ontario. There wasn't much traffic on the way, but we got our share of attention from the drivers we passed (going the opposite way) and the drivers who passed us (going the same way). A kid and what looked like a giant chicken, in a little smoking trucklike car, was not the sort of sight encountered every day in the suburbs of Rochester, New York.

Braddock Point was nice. There was a kind of park there, and we had a good view of the lake. I had never seen a Great Lake before. It looked like the ocean, which I have seen. In fact, the only difference between it and the ocean was that it was a lake, and not salty. It had waves and everything.

"And there he is, just waiting for us, taunting us because he knows we haven't got our boat, telescopes, and cameras," Professor McFwain said.

"Who? Yobgorgle?" I asked. I was getting excited.

"Who else?" Professor McFwain said. "It's

uncanny—you go out without any equipment, and there he is—just as plain as day. But go after him with a recording device, a camera, or even a reliable witness . . . not a sign of him. It's almost as if he could read your mind."

"Where? Where is he? I didn't see anything!" I was looking as hard as I could in every direction. All I could see was empty lake, except for a boat way off in the distance. It looked like some kind of a work boat; it wasn't a pleasure craft.

"He's right out there," Professor McFwain said, pointing at the boat in the distance, "big as life and twice as ugly."

"All I see is that boat," I said.

"Now you're beginning to learn a few things about the craft of monster-hunting," Professor McFwain said. "To you or any other average, untrained person, that sea monster floating on the surface out there looks like an old fishing boat or a small freighter, but that's just because your eyes aren't accustomed to scanning for monsters. I can see him as plain as the nose on your face. I can almost count his scales. I can even tell that he's asleep. Oh, if we were only in our boat! What an opportunity to get close to him and snap a picture before he wakes up!"

69

"It looks just like a boat to me," I said. "I can even see smoke coming from it."

"Now that's interesting," Professor Ambrose McFwain said. "The reason you see smoke is because you expect to see it. When you see a boat, like the one you imagine you see, you expect to see smoke—so you see it. It isn't really there, you know."

I shaded my eyes with my hand. I squinted. It still looked like a boat. In fact, it looked more like a boat. I was pretty sure it *was* a boat, but I wanted to give Professor McFwain the benefit of the doubt, so I really tried to see it as a monster. But the more I looked, the more certain I was that it was a boat. I told Professor McFwain that I thought so.

"Well, there's no substitute for experience," Professor McFwain said. "You'll get to be able to distinguish a monster from a boat, I assure you, but it will take time. For now, you'll just have to trust me. Anyway, you've had your first look at Yobgorgle, even if you aren't ready to appreciate it, and I'd say that you were a pretty lucky young man. Now, let's head back for town. There's nothing more we can do here without equipment, drat it!"

We bumped along the road back to town in

the Hindustan-eight. I was still not convinced that what we had seen was anything but a boat, but I decided that it would be best not to say anything more about it to Professor McFwain. He seemed very happy with his day's activity, and he hummed a tune as he drove.

· 11 ·

Professor McFwain went upstairs into the fat men's clothing factory and brought down the cowboy suit for Uncle Mel. It was really something. It was blue, and it had all sorts of fancy embroidery and fringes and shiny stuff on it. He also had a big round box. I guessed that had the hat in it.

"Here, Eugene, take this to your uncle with my compliments," Professor McFwain said. "I'll let you go for the day—you've had enough excitement. I'll see you tomorrow."

The cowboy suit was on a hanger and covered by one of those clear plastic bags. I carried the cowboy suit by the hanger and the box with the hat in it by the string that was attached to it, and walked back to the motel.

Uncle Mel flipped when he saw the cowboy suit. He tore his clothes off and put it on right away. It fitted him pretty good, except for the hat, which was just a tiny bit too large. He didn't seem to notice; he looked in the mirror and smiled and smiled. All he said for about fifteen minutes was, "Wow!" over and over.

The telephone rang. It was Professor Ambrose McFwain. "I wanted to know if the suit fits," he said.

"It fits perfectly," Uncle Mel said. "I'm wearing it right now."

"And have you had your evening meal?" Professor McFwain asked.

"Not yet," Uncle Mel said. "I just got back from the factory."

"Well, I suggest you keep your fancy suit on," Professor McFwain said. "I've just gotten a call from Colonel Ken Krenwinkle, the multibillionaire, and he's invited me and you and Eugene to dine with him. So if it's all right with you, I'll pick you up in ten minutes."

Uncle Mel asked me if I wanted to eat with a multibillionaire. I said it was all right with me.

He told Professor McFwain yes, and we went outside to wait for him.

After a few minutes the little green truck pulled up outside of the motel.

"Look!" Uncle Mel said. "There's a chicken driving that Hindustan-eight!"

I told him it was Professor McFwain.

"Get in! Get in!" Professor McFwain said. "We've got a long way to go, and we'll have to hurry if we don't want to be late."

Uncle Mel had some trouble getting into the little car. For one thing, he was too fat, and for another, the car wasn't high enough for him to sit in it wearing the light blue cowboy hat. He finally squeezed himself into the front seat and dragged the hat, which was somewhat crushed, in after him. He smoothed out the hat and put it on his lap. The little car leaned to the right.

"Slide over to the left as far as you can, Eugene," Professor McFwain said. "We have to trim ship—get better balance. This is good practice for when we're all out in the boat together."

"We're going out in a boat?" Uncle Mel asked.

"Yes," Professor McFwain said. "I forgot to tell you—you're invited to join the expedition

74

to hunt for Yobgorgle. That is, if you would like that."

"Gosh!" Uncle Mel said. "I'm not sure. I mean, I've always sort of wanted to have an adventure, but I've never been in a boat, and I don't know . . . I'd feel sort of awkward."

"Of course, you couldn't go monster-hunting in that beautiful suit," Professor McFwain said. "If you decide to go with us, I could arrange with my friend at the factory to make you a beautiful safari suit with lots of little pockets and flaps on the shoulders and short pants."

"Would it have a hat with a leopardskin band like Victor Mature used to wear in the movies?" Uncle Mel asked.

"Imitation leopardskin."

"I think I'd like that," Uncle Mel said. "I'd like to join the expedition and go looking for the monster, but I could only come in the evening and on the weekend."

"We'll be looking for him mostly at night," Professor McFwain said, "so that won't be a problem."

"Incidentally, Professor," Uncle Mel said, "I notice you're wearing a chicken suit. Is there any particular reason for it?"

Professor Ambrose McFwain told Uncle Mel

all about buying the Hindustan-eight from Colonel Ken Krenwinkle, and the condition that he wear the chicken suit at all times when driving it.

I had heard all this before, so I sat in the back seat, as far over to the left as I could get, and looked out the window. We had left the city and were driving through a forest. Every now and then Professor Ambrose McFwain would slow down, as if he was looking for a landmark. All I could see was trees.

Professor McFwain was telling Uncle Mel how we had seen Yobgorgle out in the lake that day. I put in that it looked like a boat to me, but neither of them paid any attention. Uncle Mel was very interested in the sighting—almost as interested as he was in Professor McFwain's description of Fred's Fat Pig. Professor McFwain promised to take Uncle Mel there soon.

"How about after dinner tonight?" Uncle Mel asked.

"We'll see," said the Professor.

Professor McFwain seemed to be counting trees now. He was driving very slowly. He stopped in front of a particularly large tree and tooted the horn.

A door opened in the side of the tree, and an

old man with white hair stepped out. "Yes, sir?" the old man said.

"Professor Ambrose McFwain and party to see Colonel Ken Krenwinkle," Professor Mc-Fwain said.

"One moment while I telephone, sir," the old man said. He stepped back into the tree. I guessed there was a telephone in there. He came out again in a minute, "It's all right, sir. I'll open the gate."

The old man went back into the tree again and must have pushed a button. Then the trees next to the big tree with the old man in it lifted up like a giant curtain! I never heard of any gate like that! They were fake trees, of course, and there must have been some giant machinery concealed in the woods to lift them like that. Professor McFwain threw the Hindustan-eight into gear, and we lurched forward.

It was twilight. I could just make out a long driveway through the trees. The Hindustan-eight's headlights flickered as we bounced along. The driveway led out of the forest, and I could see a vast lawn, with a big house in the middle of it, a long way off.

It took about five minutes to get to the end of the driveway. When we pulled up in front of

77

the house, Colonel Ken Krenwinkle was standing in the doorway.

"Good evening, gentlemen," he said. "I'm so glad you could come on such short notice."

"We are honored," Professor McFwain said. "You're already met my assistant, Eugene Winkleman, the youngest doctoral candidate ever to attend Catatonic University, and this is Doctor Pierre Unclemel, a specialist in nutritional mechanics, who has consented to join our little expedition."

I must have looked startled, for Professor McFwain turned to us and whispered. "Never mind the fibs. It's polite to do that when dealing with rich people."

"The honor is mine," Colonel Ken Krenwinkle said. "Please come in. Dinner will be ready shortly."

We went into the house, which was bigger than the Rochester Public Library.

"Let's go right into the great hall," Colonel Ken Krenwinkle said. "We can have a glass of wine and get acquainted while we wait for our meal."

The great hall was just that. It was about the biggest room I've ever seen without basketball hoops. There was a giant table in the middle of it about a block long. On the walls there were big wooden plaques with trophies on them. In movies I've seen the trophies were usually lion's heads or elephants, and maybe there were suits or armor and old swords and battle-axes. On the walls of Colonel Ken Krenwinkle's great hall were the front ends of automobiles from just behind the windshield to the head-lights. Each automobile was mounted on a polished wooden plaque, and there was a little brass nameplate at the bottom of the plaque. The cars were about fifteen feet above our heads. They looked small in the huge room. I recognized a Hindustan-eight and a few other cars I'd seen before. There were some smaller plaques with half-motorcycles and washing machines, drill presses, power lawn mowers, a popcorn vending machine from a movie house, a small cement mixer, and at the end of the great hall a forklift truck. The forklift was mounted with the two steel forks angled slightly downward, so it reminded me of an elephant. The brass nameplate underneath read, "Nafsu Motors Forklift, 44 horsepower, bagged in Utica, New York, 1962."

"As you can see from my trophies," Colonel Ken Krenwinkle said, "I don't go in for conventional game—in fact, I'm against taking the lives of wild animals—but stalking a wild forklift in the industrial parks of Utica, alone and unarmed in my modified Deuesenberg 16-cylinder safari car—that's another matter. That's true sport, gentlemen."

"I was admiring your 1952 Chrysler," Professor McFwain said.

"Ah, yes," Colonel Ken Krenwinkle said. "Bagged the blighter out west in Buffalo in '70. I had the devil of a time with that one, I don't mind telling you. I wounded the brute on my first pass, and it went berserk. Just as it charged, something went haywire with my magneto—I was stopped dead. Well, the only thing to do was to finish it off by hand. I climbed up on the hood, and just at the moment of impact, I jumped aboard, threw the monster into reverse, and ran it into a concrete embankment rear end first. It was a close one."

"Excuse me," I said. "I'm not sure I understand this. How do you go about hunting cars?"

"It's very simple, my young friend," Colonel Ken Krenwinkle said. "I locate the beast I wish to bag. Then my trusted shikaris, who have made arrangements with the owner, if any, set the throttle, get the thing in motion in a big field or other open space, and I give chase in the modified Deuesenberg. I try to finish the thing off with a clean collision. Then it's time to take photos, and off to the taxidermist to have the dents smoothed out, and up on the wall it goes."

All I could do was stare at the cars on the wall. I had never heard of anything like this.

· 12 ·

The meal served at Colonel Ken Krenwinkle's house consisted of nothing but vegetable dishes. Colonel Ken Krenwinkle was a vegetarian. There were a number of different kinds of salads and some hot vegetable dishes and different kinds of grains. I liked everything, but Uncle Mel and Professor Ambrose McFwain just nibbled and pushed things around on their plates. I was pretty certain we'd be stopping at Fred's Fat Pig later on. They just weren't used to that kind of food.

During the meal, Colonel Ken Krenwinkle told us more about his adventures hunting automobiles and other machines. Professor Mc-Fwain told stories about monster-hunting expeditions in various parts of the world. Uncle Mel told about new developments in food vending machines. Colonel Ken Krenwinkle said he'd like to bag one of the new freeze-dried, mix-and-mush, micro-wave machines for his collection of trophies. Uncle Mel said he'd find out how much they cost, and if Colonel Ken Krenwinkle wanted, the factory could probably fix the machine up with wheels and a motor so the chase would be more sporting. Colonel Ken Krenwinkle told him to go ahead and arrange it, if he could.

Everybody agreed that when Professor McFwain had finished making arrangements, we would all go out on Lake Ontario looking for the monster, Yobgorgle. Professor McFwain was going to get a safari suit for Uncle Mel at a wholesale price. Colonel Ken Krenwinkle already had a safari suit, and I didn't want one. Professor McFwain remarked that he found the chicken suit very comfortable and had gotten a lot of compliments wearing it.

"I'm glad you like it," Colonel Ken Krenwinkle said, "I had a very successful day, if I say so myself. I have three other gentlemen rid-ing around in chicken suits in small foreign cars; a life-size papier-maché cow mounted on top of a late model station wagon; a sedan with a loud speaker that plays a recording of "West End Blues" with Louis Armstrong twenty-four hours a day; and two vans fully upholstered in fake fur on the outside. It's not the best day I ever had dealing in used cars, but it was a very good day."

We all agreed that Colonel Ken Krenwinkle had certainly done well.

After the meal, Colonel Ken Krenwinkle invited us to his den for cigars and coffee. Of course, I didn't have either. I had a cherry milkshake with real cherries in it. The grown-ups smoked cigars and sat in big green leather chairs. Colonel Ken Krenwinkle's study had a lot of portraits of ducks on the walls. These weren't the usual sort of pictures of ducks. I had seen them—I don't know where—maybe in a doctor's office, with ducks in flight or maybe a close-up of a couple of ducks. These were pictures of duck's heads. The ducks had nice expressions in the pictures. I never knew ducks had expressions.

"I see you're admiring my duck pictures," Colonel Ken Krenwinkle said. "I have a soft spot in my heart for ducks of all kinds. Ducks are the major enthusiasm of my life, more so than sport, more so than making untold billions of dollars. You see, gentlemen, my mother died when I was very young, my father was away much of the time, and I was . . ." Here Colonel Ken Krenwinkle stopped speaking, overcome with emotion. "I was raised by a duck, bless her dear heart. I hope that none of you ever eats ducks, gentlemen."

Professor Ambrose McFwain and Uncle Mel both swore that they never ate ducks, which was probably true, since no fast-food chain that I know of serves duck. I had never eaten duck either, as far as I could remember, so I told Colonel Ken Krenwinkle I would never eat duck in the future, if I could get out of it.

"Thank you, gentlemen," Colonel Ken Krenwinkle said. "I knew you were all good men. I'm proud to be associated with you."

Things got quiet for a while after Colonel Ken Krenwinkle's emotional speech about ducks. Then Professor McFwain suggested that we'd better be going. I was ready for that. I figured that the Professor and Uncle Mel would be needing some junk food by this time.

"So early?" Colonel Ken Krenwinkle said. "I

had hoped you'd stay a little longer."

Professor McFwain reminded Colonel Ken Krenwinkle that I was but a youngster, and he and Uncle Mel were responsible for seeing to it that I got to bed at a decent hour.

When we went outside, the Hindustan-eight refused to start.

"Never mind," Colonel Ken Krenwinkle said. "Just leave it here. My driver will fix it for you in the morning and deliver it to your office. I will drive you home, and I have something that may be of interest to show you en route. Just excuse me for a moment while I make the arrangements."

Colonel Ken Krenwinkle went into his house and gave some instructions to his staff. In a few moments two enormous cars pulled up in front of the house. One was a shiny black Rolls Royce, the other was the longest, highest car I have ever seen. It was greenish gray, and the paint was chipped and scratched. There were wire screens over the headlights.

"We will ride in the Rolls," Colonel Ken Krenwinkle said, "and my servant will follow in the safari car. I hope you don't mind if we make a short stop on the way. It won't take very long."

Professor McFwain and Uncle Mel said they didn't mind at all. They both glanced at their watches. They were worried that they'd get back to town after McTavish's had closed. With the Hindustan-eight out of commission, Fred's Fat Pig was no longer a possibility for that evening. I could read Uncle Mel's mind when it came to food, and Professor McFwain, though crazier in other ways, wasn't much different. I didn't care. I wasn't hungry, and I wanted to see what Colonel Ken Krenwinkle was going to show us on the way home.

He drove the Rolls Royce himself. It was a neat car! Now I know why they are so expensive. They're really nice to ride in.

Colonel Ken Krenwinkle drove fast through the night. The car had a stereo that played a tape of duck noises. "We're going to make a stop at the County Fair Grounds in Henrietta, a suburb of Rochester," Colonel Ken Krenwinkle said. "Arrangements have been made for some time—I was just waiting for a fine night like this."

When we arrived at the deserted fair grounds, Colonel Ken Krenwinkle's servant jumped out of the safari car and ran off somewhere. In a few seconds, banks of floodlights switched on, revealing a little green car at the far end of the fair grounds.

"There it is!" Colonel Ken Krenwinkle said. He was very excited, "A 1969 Austin America in perfect condition. I had to search everywhere for it. Just stay here, you'll be perfectly safe."

Colonel Ken Krenwinkle jumped out of the Rolls Royce, and ran over to his modified Deuesenberg safari car, hopped in, and gunned the motor.

In the distance, the 1969 Austin America started with a puff of gray smoke. We could just see that there was someone behind the wheel. The Austin started moving, and Colonel Ken Krenwinkle's driver jumped out of the moving car and ran away. Colonel Ken Krenwinkle revved the motor of the modified Deuesenberg safari car but didn't move.

The Austin was picking up speed. It was weaving and turning and going in little circles. Then it straightened out and started moving toward us. It got closer. I was scared. I wanted to look over and see what Colonel Ken Krenwinkle was doing, but I couldn't take my eyes off the Austin speeding toward the three of us in the Rolls Royce.

The Austin wasn't more than thirty feet away when he heard a loud roar. Colonel Ken Krenwinkle had popped the clutch of his safari car, and was coming toward us in a cloud of dust. For a while it looked as if we were going to be hit by both the Austin and the Deuesenberg at the same time, but at the last moment, Colonel Ken Krenwinkle veered off to the left, just enough to miss us, and caught the Austin by the left front fender as he passed in front of it. The Austin spun around and began going in the other direction. Colonel Ken Krenwinkle was making a wide circle. He continued turning and caught the Austin amidships as he came around 180 degrees.

The Austin left the ground, flew sideways fifteen or twenty feet, and landed on its four wheels with a crash. It shuddered, and then was still. Colonel Ken Krenwinkle came to a stop a little to the right of the Austin, got out of his safari car, and walked over to the smoking wreck. His driver ran up with a camera and took a flash picture of him. Then he walked back to the Rolls Royce.

"Bravo! Bravo!" shouted Uncle Mel and the Professor, when Colonel Ken Krenwinkle returned to the Rolls Royce.

"Oh, it was nothing," Colonel Ken Krenwinkle said. "Not very dangerous, but I thought you might enjoy seeing how it's done."

When we got back to Rochester, McTavish's was already closed. The only place open was Bob's Beanery. Of course, Uncle Mel and Professor Ambrose McFwain didn't tell Colonel Ken Krenwinkle that they were going there. They didn't want him to know that they hadn't enjoyed his dinner. He dropped us all off in front of the motel, and we walked to Bob's Beanery.

· 13 ·

Bob's Beanery looked sort of different at night. The neon lights in the window and the fluorescent lights on the ceiling made everything look greenish. There were a few people sitting at the counter and one guy sleeping with his head on his arms at one of the tables.

Uncle Mel, Professor McFwain, and I sat down at a table.

"This is nice. We'll get a nice breeze here," said Professor McFwain.

They ordered hamburgers. I ordered a cherry cola. It was interesting that nobody in Bob's Beanery seemed to take any special notice of a man in a chicken suit and another in a very loud cowboy suit sitting in a lunchroom late at night. Either people in Rochester are very polite, or they're very hard to surprise.

"That was exciting," Uncle Mel said, "when Colonel Ken Krenwinkle went after the Austin."

"Yes, he's a brave man," Professor McFwain said. "He's just the sort of fellow one would want to face a monster with."

"I was thinking about that," Uncle Mel said. "I've never done anything brave. The only sort of hunting I've ever done is shooting clay pigeons. I wonder if *I'm* the sort of man one would want to face a monster with."

"Why, my dear fellow, of course you are," Professor McFwain said. "The only reason you've never done anything brave is you haven't had an opportunity. I can see you now, wearing your brand-new safari suit. . . ."

"And the hat with the imitation leopardskin band," Uncle Mel put in.

". . . and the hat with the imitation leopardskin band," Professor McFwain said. "What a dashing fellow you'll be!"

"I'll never know until I've tried," Uncle Mel said.

"That's right!" Professor McFwain said. "I've known brave men and adventurers on every continent—I can tell when a man has got the right stuff in him for daring deeds—and I'm sure you'll be just fine."

"Really?"

"Really. You'll see for yourself when we put out in the lake tomorrow night."

"Tomorrow night?" That took Uncle Mel and me by surprise. "Are we going out after Yobgorgle tomorrow night?" we both asked at once.

"I can't see any reason why not," Professor McFwain said. "I'll send a message to Colonel Ken Krenwinkle when his driver brings my car, and we'll all meet at my office at eight o'clock sharp. Then we'll motor out to Irondequoit Bay with the research vessel in tow and put in a couple of hours of searching. Then a light snack, and another good day's work will be done—unless we find him, of course."

"What if we do find him?" I asked.

"Well, the main thing is to try to get pictures," Professor McFwain said. "After that, it's up to the monster."

"But will my safari suit be ready in time?" Uncle Mel wanted to know.

"Just leave that to me," Professor McFwain

said. "It will be ready for you, hat and all, when you come to my office at eight. They turn them out like cupcakes. You'd never believe there were so many fat explorers."

"Do you want me to turn up in the morning?" I asked Professor Ambrose McFwain.

"Not necessary, my boy," he said. "I plan to sleep as late as possible in order to be fresh for our adventure in the evening. I suggest you do the same. Just come at eight o'clock with the others."

"I guess we'd better break this up so we can get some rest," Uncle Mel said.

"Good idea," said Professor McFwain. "We'll have one more round of double cheeseburgers and call it a night." He ordered two more double-deluxe cheeseburgers with everything.

"Two more doubles for the cowboy and the chicken!" the man behind the counter shouted into the kitchen.

· 14 ·

The next day dragged on and on. I tried to sleep as late as I could, which wasn't very late. I was wide awake at dawn thinking about going out in the lake after Yobgorgle. I tried to go back to sleep and didn't go out to McTavish's for breakfast with Uncle Mel, but it didn't work. I got dressed and went outside into the street.

It was going to be some hot day—it was hot at nine in the morning. I didn't feel like going to McTavish's now that Uncle Mel wasn't with me, and I had a choice. Bob's Beanery had lost some of its charm too. I wandered around looking for a new place to eat. I found one. It was

95

called Charlie's Health Food and Juice Bar. The thing that attracted me to it was the window display. There was a mechanical carrot about four feet tall, with arms and legs, who kept lowering himself into a giant juice-making machine. There was a sign that said COOLER INSIDE. I went inside. If it was cooler, it wasn't more than two degrees cooler. There was an electric fan, like the one in Bob's Beanery, but it just didn't seem to be able to do the job.

However, Charlie's Health Food and Juice Bar was truly a great place! They had carrot juice! I never had carrot juice before. Charlie— that was the guy who owned the place—told me that if you drink a whole lot of carrot juice you'll turn orange. I had three glasses—not enough to turn me orange. I also had a couple of these nifty health-food muffins, with all kinds of grains and ground-up stuff and nuts in them. A really magnificent breakfast! I decided to eat in Charlie's Health Food and Juice Bar every morning. That meant eating without Uncle Mel—it wasn't the sort of place you could drag him into.

Charlie told me to come back for lunch. I said I would. Then I drifted over to the library. I went into the secret room and leafed through a book about a kid who gets involved with an old maniac and a bunch of talking lizards, but I really couldn't get interested. I was too nervous waiting for it to be time to meet Professor Ambrose McFwain and go out looking for the sea monster.

I ate my lunch in Charlie's place. He told me about bran and vitamin B-complex, and brewers' yeast. Charlie was an interesting guy. He knew a lot about food and what it does for you. More than ever, I wondered how Uncle Mel and Professor McFwain could stay alive, eating what they did. I asked Charlie. He said that sometimes your diet takes a long time to catch up with you.

I walked around and looked at the river and looked into store windows. I just couldn't get anything organized. Finally, it got too hot to be outside, and I went back to the motel and watched soap operas on television until Uncle Mel came home from work at the factory. He sent me over to Professor McFwain's to see if his safari suit was ready. He said he couldn't wait until eight o'clock.

Professor McFwain was sleeping on a folding cot in his office when I arrived. He didn't want to wake up; he just pointed to the suit, which was hanging from the doorknob in a plastic garment bag, and said, "See you at eight."

I brought the suit back to the motel. Uncle Mel was in the shower. He came out and put on the suit. After looking at himself in the mirror for a long time, he said, "Now let's go out and have some dinner."

"You're not going out in the street dressed like that?" I said.

"Why not?" Uncle Mel said.

It occurred to me that I had been seen in the street with a guy wearing a cowboy suit and a guy dressed up as a chicken. A fat man in a Jungle-Jim suit was no worse. We went out.

Even Uncle Mel likes a change once in a while, so we didn't go to McTavish's. We went to Burger-Chief, which was introducing a new Swiss-steak sandwich. Uncle Mel had read an advertisement in the newspaper and wanted to try it. It was close to uneatable. It was sort of a toy steak. It looked like a piece of meat, but I couldn't tell what it was. It was on a toy roll that looked like a real roll with a crust and little seeds, but it was all stamped from one piece of something or other. Uncle Mel didn't like the steak sandwich either. He only ate three. He says you can never be sure if you like something until you've had it three times.

Walking away from the Burger-Chief, Uncle Mel said that he felt a little sick. I wasn't surprised. I felt very sick, and I had only eaten about half of one of those plastic steaks.

It was almost eight when we arrived at the fat men's clothing factory. Colonel Ken Krenwinkle was already there, standing on the sidewalk with Professor McFwain. The research vessel was on a little trailer tied to the back of the Hindustan-eight with a piece of rope. We all got into the car and drove out to the place where Professor McFwain intended to start the night's search.

We put the research vessel into the water. It was the same rowboat we had seen in the movie. Professor McFwain got in first, and then me, and then Colonel Ken Krenwinkle. The boat was sitting fairly low in the water. Uncle Mel got in. Colonel Ken Krenwinkle and Professor McFwain started to row. They didn't seem to be able to get the boat moving. The sky was still fairly light, and I could see the water glisten as it poured over the sides of the boat. It filled up in a few seconds and then slid out from under us. We floundered around for a few more seconds and then discovered we could stand up—the water was only about four feet deep.

We sloshed around for a while, trying to find the boat with our feet, but we couldn't seem to make contact with it. Besides it was getting dark. Finally, we all slogged out of the water, back to the Hindustan-eight.

Professor McFwain was mad. Uncle Mel was worried. He felt guilty about being the one to swamp the boat, and he was worried that his explorer suit might be ruined. Colonel Ken Krenwinkle seemed to be in good spirits, though. "Ah, yes," he said, "the frustrations and setbacks of the chase. This is what real adventure is all about. Now we'll have to use our wits—and improvise—and see what we can come up with!"

"I don't see what we can improvise," Professor McFwain said. "The McFwain Foundation research vessel appears to be lost. We can't go after a sea monster without a boat. What do you suggest in the way of improvising?"

"Well," said Colonel Ken Krenwinkle, "how about an eighty-two-foot yacht? My private craft is anchored about a hundred yards away. It was going to be a surprise. I had instructed my crew to follow us, and then when we were finished searching, we were all to go on board, take the research vessel in tow, and have some refreshments. I suppose we could search from the yacht."

"Well, it's not quite the same as the research vessel," Professor McFwain said.

"But it'll do in an emergency," Colonel Ken Krenwinkle said.

"You're right!" Professor McFwain said. "We have to use the resources at our disposal. Lead us to the yacht, Colonel."

Colonel Ken Krenwinkle took a little thing that looked like a transistor radio out of his pocket. He pulled out a telescoping antenna and pressed a red button. The little gadget made a continuous series of beeping noises, and out of the darkness came the biggest, whitest boat I've ever seen.

· 15 ·

Colonel Ken Krenwinkle's boat was called *La Forza Materiale*. Professor McFwain asked him what the boat's name meant, and Colonel Ken Krenwinkle told him that he'd tell him later. As far as I know, he never did. The boat was really fancy. It had lots of polished wood and shiny brass and white paint. Everything was clean and smooth and shiny. The engine made a deep, even humming noise. It was some fancy boat.

"Professor McFwain," Colonel Ken Krenwinkle said, "I'd like you to meet the captain of *La Forza Materiale*, a great sailor and a fine gentleman. His name is Sinbad Weinstein. While you are aboard, Captain Sinbad Weinstein will take orders directly from you. Please treat this boat as your own research vessel."

Captain Sinbad Weinstein was a very tall fellow with a neatly trimmed beard and eyeglasses. He bowed to Professor McFwain and said, "It is a pleasure to meet you. I await your instructions."

Professor McFwain reached into his pocket and took out a bunch of little aluminum whistles. He distributed them to Colonel Ken Krenwinkle, Captain Sinbad Weinstein, Uncle Mel, and me. "I have more of these for your crew, Captain," he said. "These are ultra high-frequency dog whistles. Their sound is of too high a frequency for the human ear to hear. Ordinarily, only dogs can hear them. However, I have perfected this, the McFwain high-frequency ear stopple." He showed us a pair of white plastic things that looked like badminton shuttlecocks. Professor McFwain sort of screwed one into each ear. They stuck out strangely, making him look like some sort of strange bird—all the more because he was still wearing his chicken suit, except for the headpiece, which had gotten lost, probably when the research vessel sank.

"With these," he said, "I will be able to hear the high-frequency whistles I have given to each of you. In this way, you will be able to signal me and, hopefully, not alarm the monster, if we are lucky enough to sight him."

I wondered how Professor Ambrose McFwain knew that Yobgorgle couldn't hear high-frequency sounds.

"What I propose is this," he went on. "We will darken ship as much as the law allows, leaving only the required red and green marker lights to prevent collision. Then we will position ourselves around the rail, each man looking in a different direction. I'm a little worried about the engine noise—I'll ask Captain Sinbad Weinstein to drift as much as possible. It would have been better in the McFwain Foundation Research vessel, with no engine, of course. If you think you've sighted the monster, you will blow your whistle. No one will hear it—but with my high-frequency ear stopples, I will hear it—and I will come running with my infrared camera for night photography and take pictures of the monster. We will begin with a two-hour watch, during which time no one will speak or make any noise at all."

"At the conclusion of the watch," Colonel

Ken Krenwinkle interrupted, "we can gather in the main cabin for some refreshments prepared by the ship's cook."

"Thank you," Professor McFwain said.

The two-hour watch began. My station was on the left side of the boat—the port side, Professor McFwain called it—toward the back, or stern. There were several crew members in white coats, who appeared and vanished silently, and one of them brought me a wood and canvas chair to sit in. We churned out toward the middle of the lake. After a while, the *La Forza Materiale*'s engines were switched off and the boat drifted silently. It had clouded over—no moon, no stars. The darkness was total, except for the dim glow of the boat's marker lights. Now and then I could see a light twinkling on shore. A lot of the time I couldn't see anything. I held up my hand in front of my face. I couldn't see it. I had never been in such darkness. The only sound was the water sloshing against the sides of the boat.

Sitting in my chair, I tried to look for Yobgorgle. It was hard to look for something when I couldn't see anything. After a while, I couldn't be sure if I was awake or asleep. I might have been dreaming. I actually had to feel my eyes from time to time to make sure they were open.

I liked being on the boat. I even liked the way the lake smelled, though it was not as fresh as I would have imagined. I liked the rocking sensation and the noises the water made. It was very peaceful.

A couple of times I heard someone cough softly or clear his throat. Except for that, there was no noise aboard the *La Forza Materiale*.

After a long time, the darkness got lighter. That is, I started seeing it as lighter. It was still totally dark. I still couldn't see anything. It was just my eyes getting more and more used to the darkness. Now, instead of blackness, I saw grayness. I couldn't see the water. It had been a long time since I had seen a light from shore. Either we were too far away to see any lights and the boat was drifting toward the middle of Lake Ontario, or I was facing away from shore.

I couldn't tell how much time had passed. I couldn't tell if I had been watching for Yobgorgle for an hour or for ten minutes.

Then I saw something. That is, I thought that maybe I saw something. I didn't actually *see* something. It was just a darker place in the darkness. It didn't have a shape. It didn't have a size. I couldn't tell how far or near it was. I wasn't even sure I was seeing it. I tried to open my eyes wide to see it better, but I couldn't be sure. It was there sometimes, and sometimes it wasn't.

I thought about blowing my whistle, but I wasn't sure there was anything out there. I decided to wait and see if it got any clearer. It did. It got closer. It got bigger. Soon I was sure that something was out there, floating near our boat. I thought that probably it was a small island—it was too large to be another boat. I still couldn't make out a definite shape, but there was *something* out there. I blew the whistle and kept blowing it until Professor McFwain, making no noise, came up behind me.

"Where?" he whispered.

"There," I whispered.

"Take my hand and point," he whispered.

I pointed his hand at the black mass. "Yes," Professor McFwain whispered. "I think I do see something."

I heard the camera click. I didn't see any light, because the camera had a special infrared light that you can't see without special glasses.

"That should do it," Professor McFwain whispered. "Now, I'll take one with the regular flash, just to make sure."

The light of the flashbulb seemed to last a long time. I was looking at the black mass, hoping I would get a glimpse of whatever it was when Professor McFwain snapped the picture.

I did get a glimpse of something. It was big—bigger than I had guessed—much bigger than *La Forza Materiale*. It was pink! There was something enormous and pink and rounded and shiny floating in the water about the distance of a city block from the boat!

"I'll tell Captain Sinbad Weinstein to turn on the searchlights," Professor McFwain said aloud, "although I have no doubt that the flash scared him off. Still, we've got the picture—if it only comes out this time—and you've seen him, Eugene, my boy. You and I have seen Yobgorgle!"

When the searchlights came on and made long, thin, gray cones through the blackness, the thing had *not* gone away! It was still there, shining pinkly in the searchlight's beams. It was unmistakable. Anybody could have seen in a moment that what we were looking at was an enormous, impossible, gigantic, floating pink pig!

· 16 ·

Everybody gathered at the rail and stared at the thing. It was a pig—there was no mistaking it.

"And that," asked Colonel Ken Krenwinkle, "that is Yobgorgle?"

"I confess, I am as amazed as you are," Professor Ambrose McFwain said. "I had no idea that Yobgorgle was so . . . so . . . porciform."

"Porciform?" Uncle Mel said.

"Yes, shaped like a pig," Professor McFwain said. "This goes against all the rules of Monsterology. By rights, he should be like a scaly dragon or a walrus with three eyes—something bizarre. But, as you can see, he is just an ordinary-looking barnyard pig, fifteen or twenty times larger than normal."

"I should say that's nothing to be disappointed about," said Captain Sinbad Weinstein. "Pigs that size don't grow on trees."

"Of course, you're right," said Professor McFwain. "I'm just trying to get used to the idea. Captain, the monster doesn't seem to have noticed us. Do you think we can get a little closer?"

Captain Sinbad Weinstein started the engines as quietly as he could. We made slow progress in the direction of the monster. The floating pig gave no sign that it was aware of us.

"You'd think that the searchlights would have scared him," I said.

"He may be asleep," Uncle Mel said.

That was the only explanation. As we got closer and closer, the pig did not move. It was bigger than any of us had thought. It was considerably more than twenty times larger than an ordinary barnyard pig. I was getting a little nervous about being so close to anything that big.

Apparently Uncle Mel was having the same thought. "Don't you think we're close enough?" he asked. At this point, the pig was towering over us.

"Nonsense!" said Colonel Ken Krenwinkle. "This is the best sport I've had since I bagged the Mack truck in Herkimer County. I want to get close enough to touch the fellow!"

Professor McFwain didn't say anything. He was busy snapping pictures. Captain Sinbad Weinstein seemed perfectly happy in the wheelhouse. It was about this time that I noticed that the members of the crew of *La Forza Materiale* had lowered a lifeboat and were rowing away as fast as they could.

"Look!" I shouted. "The crew is running away!"

"Not so loud, boy!" Professor McFwain said. "We don't want to wake Yobgorgle up until we're right on top of him. Then I can get some action closeups."

"That crew is a cowardly lot," Colonel Ken Krenwinkle said. "I'm going to take something out of their wages for this, you can be sure."

"I wish the crew had told me what they were going to do," Uncle Mel said. "I would have gone with them. Don't you all think we've gotten close enough? Professor McFwain, you've gotten some really wonderful pictures. Let's go a little distance away so we can watch the monster. Maybe we'll get to see him feeding.

Wouldn't you like to know what he eats?"

"I think he eats boats," I said. "Big ones. Please, let's get out of here."

"What's this?" Colonel Ken Krenwinkle said. "Let's not panic. The worst thing with big game is to let them know you're afraid of them—they can smell it. Look him in the eye—don't let him get the better of you."

We were close enough now to bounce a tennis ball off the pig's snout. He still hadn't moved or paid the least attention to us. I was hoping that maybe he was dead, when I realized that I could hear him breathing. He was breathing or snoring or maybe growling. It was a continuous grinding noise. It sounded more mechanical than piglike. Also, I could smell him. I don't have much experience with farm animals, but I know that pigs aren't supposed to smell like diesel fuel. This pig smelled like a truck—sort of a hot oil smell.

Then a voice came from the pig. "What ship are you?" the voice shouted.

Uncle Mel and Professor Ambrose McFwain and Colonel Ken Krenwinkle and Captain Sinbad Weinstein and I looked at each other.

"What ship, where from, and where bound?" the voice repeated.

"I am *La Forza Materiale*, out of Rochester, on a research expedition," Captain Sinbad Weinstein shouted through his cupped hands. "The crew has deserted. We're carrying a party of scientists and provisions for three days: imitation vegetarian hard salami, swiss cheese, whole wheat bread, pickles, cole slaw, celery tonic, mayonnaise, coffee, and non-dairy creamer; also five dozen assorted doughnuts and crullers."

Apparently this was some kind of nautical courtesy—when you meet another ship (or, in this case, a floating pig that talks to you) you're supposed to tell where you're from, what you're doing, and what you have on board.

"No corned beef?" asked the voice from the pig.

"No corned beef," Captain Sinbad Weinstein shouted. "Only what I told you. And what— uh—what pig are you?"

"I am the submarine *Flying Piggie*," the voice replied, "on a secret mission. I am the master of this vessel, Captain Van Straaten. If you wish, you may come aboard.

It was a submarine! It wasn't a real pig. It was a boat made to look just like a real pig, only much bigger. As we realized this, a hatch opened in the middle of the pig's back—just where the slot would be on a piggy bank—and a man climbed out. He was tall and wore a fancy sea captain's coat with gold braid at the cuffs. He had a great big gray beard.

"Gentlemen," the captain of the pig-submarine said, "you are the first people I have encountered after seven years of sailing this lake. Please honor me by coming on board and dining with me."

· 17 ·

We will be honored to come aboard, Captain Van Straaten," Captain Sinbad Weinstein said. "However, we can't all come at once. As I mentioned before, my crew has deserted, and at least one of us will have to stay aboard the *La Forza Materiale* to keep ship."

"That won't be necessary, Captain," said Captain Van Straaten. "Just tie up to the ring in the *Flying Piggie*'s nose. In this calm sea, there won't be any trouble. Meanwhile, I'll lower a ladder."

Captain Sinbad Weinstein tied a rope to the ring in the nose of the *Flying Piggie*, and Captain Van Straaten lowered a flexible ladder down the side of the pig-submarine. One by one, we went down the flight of stairs on the side of *La Forza Materiale* and clambered up the smooth pink side of the *Flying Piggie*. As each one of us got to the top of the ladder, Captain Van Straaten shook hands and introduced himself again. Then he directed each of us to climb into the hatch, down the ladder, and wait for him to join us.

I was the last one on board except for Captain Sinbad Weinstein, who was right behind me.

"I'll be down in a moment, gentlemen," Captain Van Straaten called down the ladder. "I just have to do a couple of things on deck, and then I'll give you a tour of the boat."

Uncle Mel, Professor Ambrose McFwain, Colonel Ken Krenwinkle, Captain Sinbad Weinstein, and I were all gathered in a little room at the bottom of the ladder. There wasn't anything in the room. The walls were made of steel plate, painted gray. There was a bronze plaque attached to one of the walls:

Deutsches Unterseeschwimmschweinboot
FLIEGENDES SCHWEIN
In Dienst gestellt, 194__

I asked Professor McFwain if he could read the writing on the plaque. He said it was in German. It said, "German Underwaterswimmingpigboat, *Flying Piggie*, Commissioned, 194__."

Captain Van Straaten came down the ladder, fastening the hatch behind him. "Are you from Germany?" I asked him.

"No, I am Dutch," he said, "but my boat was built in Germany. It is an interesting story. Perhaps you gentlemen have noticed that this submarine looks exactly like a pig."

Everyone had noticed that.

"Well, this boat was built for the German Navy right at the close of World War II. They had the idea of building submarines to look like familiar barnyard animals. In this way, if sighted by a hostile ship, the sub would be taken for a pig out for a swim, and no further notice would be taken. At a great distance, the fact that the pig was nearly a city block long would go unnoticed."

"Brilliant," said Professor McFwain.

"Yes, it was a good idea," Captain Van Straaten continued, "but the German Navy never had a chance to try it out. The war ended before they could commission their first animal-shaped submarine, the *Flying Piggie*. In fact, the *Flying Piggie* was never even assembled. It was built in the Peugeot car works in occupied France, packed in thousands of boxes, and shipped by rail to the sea where it was supposed to be put together. Years after the war, I bought the submarine, still packed in thousands of boxes, from a French junk dealer named Sharnopol. In my spare time, I assembled the sub—by this time I had come to live in America—and finally launched it in Lake Ontario exactly fourteen years ago."

"Fourteen years ago was when the first reports of Yobgorgle started to come in!" Professor McFwain shouted.

"Yes, Professor McFwain, I know about your search for the monster Yobgorgle," Captain Van Straaten said. "There is a drive-in movie in a suburb of Rochester that has a screen facing the lake. I saw the movie in which you appear by periscope two weeks ago. I hope you are not disappointed to find that your sea monster is actually an electric boat."

"Well, really, this is about the biggest success of my career," Professor McFwain said. "I mean, even if the monster isn't a prehistoric creature, at least I've found *something*."

"But what are you doing in this boat?" Captain Sinbad Weinstein asked.

"I'll be happy to answer all your questions at dinner," Captain Van Straaten said, "but now, I'd like to show you around my boat. I'm sure you'll find it interesting."

Captain Van Straaten had made a lot of improvements in the design of the *Flying Piggie*. He had no crew. Everything was done by computer and electric motors. Also he had fixed up the crew's quarters into a really nice apartment for himself.

"Gentlemen, we are now in the midsection of the boat where the spareribs would be—just a little joke," Captain Van Straaten said. "If you will make yourselves comfortable, I will go and see about the dinner. There are brandy and cigars for those who use them. I'll be right back."

Captain Van Straaten stepped out of the room and closed the door behind him. We heard a loud click.

"Well, what an interesting boat," Colonel Ken Krenwinkle said.

"And what a nice man Captain Van Straaten is," Uncle Mel said.

"I think he's locked us in this room," I said.

119

· 18 ·

Nobody seemed to pay any attention to what I'd said. Uncle Mel was spreading some cheese on a cracker he had found on a side table. Professor McFwain was munching little bits of salami. Colonel Ken Krenwinkle and Captain Sinbad Weinstein were lighting up cigars. I went to the door and tried it. "It's locked," I said.

"Eugene," Captain Sinbad Weinstein said, "submarines have watertight doors between compartments. It isn't locked, it just hard to open. I'll show you." Captain Sinbad Weinstein went to the door and tried to turn the big wheel in the middle. "It's locked," he said.

There was a noise, a humming, vibrating sort of noise, and we felt one end of the room tilt downward. "Excuse me, Captain Weinstein," Colonel Ken Krenwinkle said. "Am I correct in assuming that Captain Van Straaten has started the engines, and this boat is under way?"

"Not only that, Colonel," said Captain Sinbad Weinstein. "I believe we're diving."

"Gentlemen, please do not be alarmed," we heard Captain Van Straaten's voice say—it was coming over a loud-speaker. "It has been necessary for me to cast off from your vessel and submerge. You are all perfectly safe. Please make yourselves comfortable, and I will rejoin you in a few moments and answer all your questions. By the way, in case you are considering an act of force, I should tell you that this submarine is extremely complicated to operate—it is unlike any other boat in the world, and I am the only person who knows how to operate it. If anything should happen to me, it is very unlikely that you would ever be able to get to the surface again."

"I should say that things are getting serious," Colonel Ken Krenwinkle said.

"Let's not be hasty," Professor Ambrose

McFwain said. "Let's give Captain Van Straaten a chance to explain."

"Yes," said Captain Sinbad Weinstein. "After all, he is a ship's captain—he must be a gentleman."

"I want to get out of here," Uncle Mel said.

"So do I," I said.

Captain Van Straaten entered the room. "Ah, gentlemen, please excuse all these interruptions. Now we will be able to sit down and have something to eat and a nice talk. By the way, we're now cruising at forty knots at a depth of thirty feet."

"Good Lord!" said Captain Sinbad Weinstein. "That's terribly fast. Shouldn't you be at a porthole or a radar screen looking out for obstacles?"

"Not at all, Captain," said Captain Van Straaten. "As I told you, this is unlike any other boat in the world. It runs itself electronically. If an object should appear in our path, the *Flying Piggie* will automatically correct course and miss it. Now, please allow me to serve some food."

Captain Van Straaten opened a cupboard and took out various dishes of food and put them on the table. There was sliced roast beef, salad, two kinds of bread, pie and ice cream, wine, and a pitcher of milk. "Eat hearty, gentlemen," said Captain Van Straaten, helping us to food.

Uncle Mel took a big bite of roast beef and then screwed up his face in a strange expression. Professor Ambrose McFwain bit into a forkful of salad and stared at Uncle Mel.

"Good, isn't it?" Captain Van Straaten said. "Now I'm going to amaze you. Every single thing you're eating—everything, even the milk—is made entirely from fish. That's right—fish. This submarine was designed to be entirely self-sufficient for long periods of time. There's an incredibly efficient food-processing plant on board that can duplicate almost any taste and texture of food, using only the fish I net in my electrically operated fish-catcher."

I took a sip of milk. It tasted like fish. So did the roast beef. So did the salad and the bread. The idea of fish-flavored ice cream was too much for me, so I didn't try it.

"There are many more marvels aboard this boat, and I will tell you about all of them as the days go by," said Captain Van Straaten. "We'll have a wonderful time, don't you fear. I couldn't have asked for a more perfect crew."

"Crew?" we asked. "As the days go by?"

"Yes," said Captain Van Straaten. "I neglected to tell you that we will all be together for some considerable time—seven years at least—so we may as well be friendly."

"See here, Captain," said Colonel Ken Krenwinkle, half rising. "I think you'd better explain yourself."

"I shall be happy to explain everything," said Captain Van Straaten. "Kindly sit down and enjoy your cigar, which, by the way, is also a fish product."

Colonel Ken Krenwinkle took the cigar out of his mouth and stared at it.

"Now," said Captain Van Straaten, "kindly let me tell my story without interruption. If you have any questions when I've finished, I will be happy to answer them."

"Have you ever heard of the Flying Dutchman?" Captain Van Straaten said, lighting up a fish-cigar. "Well, I am that very person. In the version of the story you usually hear, the Flying Dutchman is captain of a cursed ship, doomed to sail the seas forever, never putting into port. Every seven years, he may touch land, but unless a woman will offer to marry him, even though it means her death, he has to continue sailing."

Captain Van Straaten took a long puff on the cigar. "That's the story most people know, and like most stories, it is not exactly accurate. In fact, I am sailing under a curse, and in fact, I do have to sail the seas—or in the present case, Lake Ontario—continually. However, I have no wish to get married, and if I did, it wouldn't make any difference to the curse, except that in addition to everything else, I'd have to drag a wife along with me. What's more, I can *never* touch land—not until the curse is lifted. You see, it's a lot more complicated than the usual story."

"Tell us more about this curse," Colonel Ken Krenwinkle said.

"Well, for one thing," said the Captain, "it is not the ship that is cursed—it is me. In the past six hundred years, I've been the captain of perhaps two dozen ships. As soon as I set foot on a ship, the curse takes over—that ship can never touch land. In order to escape the curse, I have to meet two conditions: first, I have to leave my ship and go directly to land. This might seem simple—I could just steer close to land and jump off—but in fact, no ship with me on board can come closer than five miles to any land, and I can't swim. Second, after getting ashore, if no one offers me a decent corned-beef sandwich within twenty-four hours, I have to put out to sea again. This makes going ashore in most parts of the world a futile exercise. You may ask why I don't jump off with a life-preserver and just paddle to shore. I tried that, but under the terms of the curse, anything that keeps me afloat is regarded as a ship. I spent two years floating around in a life-preserver until I finally got picked up by a ship, which then, of course, became my ship."

Uncle Mel interrupted Captain Van Straaten. "But what do you want with us? Why have you kidnapped us?"

"Because I'm lonely, man! Can't you understand that? I'm always losing crews, and then I have to sail around all by myself," Captain Van Straaten shouted. "Now that I have you jolly crewmen on board, we can have all sorts of fun. We can sing sea chanties and dance hornpipes and play games and sit around having discussions like this."

"But what if we don't want to sail in this boat forever?" I said.

"So what," said the Flying Dutchman. "Who wants to sail forever? Do you think I like it?"

"But that isn't fair," I said.

"Of course not," Captain Van Straaten said. "But is it fair that I have to sail and sail and sail with nobody to talk to?" At this point he got very excited and rushed out of the room, locking the door behind him.

· 19 ·

Well, what do you think?" Colonel Ken Krenwinkle asked Professor Ambrose McFwain, when Captain Van Straaten had left. "Is he crazy or is he really the Flying Dutchman?"

"He is certainly crazy," Professor McFwain said, "and he may also be the Flying Dutchman. In any case, I suggest we try to be as pleasant as possible and keep him calm. He strikes me as the sort of person one doesn't want to stir up."

"What about the story that he put this submarine together from parts in little boxes?" I asked. "If that's true, then it doesn't fit his story about being cursed."

"I wouldn't say anything about it, Eugene," Professor McFwain said. "Just be friendly and go along with things. We'll have to wait and see what favorable opportunity develops."

Captain Van Straaten came back. "Excuse me gentlemen," he said. "I suddenly remembered something I had to do. Now, let's continue our little chat." Captain Van Straaten looked strange—his eyes were red, and his beard was all messy. It looked as though he had been crying.

"Captain, you said you would show us the rest of this boat," Professor McFwain said.

"Yes," Captain Van Straaten said. "Do you all promise you won't try to take over my boat by force?"

We promised.

"Then I'll be happy to show you around," the Flying Dutchman said. "Please come this way."

We followed Captain Van Straaten down a long corridor. "These are the crew's quarters," he said. He showed us a small compartment hung with five hammocks. "I'm sorry the accommodations aren't more comfortable," said Captain Van Straaten, "but you are free to visit in my quarters, which are much nicer—and you can make fish-popcorn in the galley, and you can look through the periscope—oh, you'll have a good time on board the *Flying Piggie*, I promise you."

The idea of spending the rest of my life on a submarine and eating fish-popcorn didn't appeal to me at all, but I didn't say anything.

"Now this is the control room," Captain Van Straaten said. "As I explained to you before, the boat can be run electronically—that is, it can run itself—or I can steer her and control her. The only thing I can't make the boat do is get closer than five miles to any land—the curse, you know. But I can dive, run on the surface, stop, and go as fast as I like."

"Captain Van Straaten," Captain Sinbad Weinstein said, "you told us that the boat is now running at forty knots underwater. That's almost fifty miles per hour, land speed, and terribly fast for any sort of vessel—especially underwater."

"Oh, she can go much faster than that," Captain Van Straaten said. "In fact, I don't really know how fast she can go. I once had her up to ninety-three knots, and the engines weren't even working hard. She's the fastest pig afloat."

"That's way over a hundred miles an hour!"

Captain Sinbad Weinstein said. "That's faster than anything but a rocket-powered speedboat! What sort of engines does this boat have, and what do they run on?"

"They are special engines," Captain Van Straaten said, "and they run on fish-juice, which I process myself from my daily catch. As I told you the *Flying Piggie* is totally self-sufficient. As long as there are fish, she runs, and I have a thirty-day reserve of fish juice."

Captain Van Straaten led us to another compartment. "Now let me show you my traveling factory," he said. "This is where fish from Lake Ontario are converted into all the things I need for my very civilized life."

We were led into a room full of shining stainless steel pipes and vats with lots of dials and gauges and knobs and buttons.

"It looks very complicated," Captain Van Straaten said, "and it is, but it is simple to work. The *Flying Piggie* has automatic sensors located on the outside of her hull. When we encounter any fish, large or small—or any schools of fish—special nets shoot out from the sides of the boat and catch them. They are drawn into this factory-room and held for processing. If I am running low, on any stores—say cigars—I

131

just punch these keys, and the supplies I need will appear on this screen."

Captain Van Straaten pressed keys on what looked like a typewriter keyboard. "See? Just as I thought—we're down to our last box of fish cigars. Notice the numbers and letters following the listing for cigars? That's a code. I just punch up that code, like this. . . ."

Captain Van Straaten typed out the series of numbers and letters that followed the word "cigars" on the screen. There was a hissing noise. Then there was a clanking noise, and various lights flashed on and off. After a minute or two, a stainless steel door opened in the side of a large boxlike thing, and let out a cloud of fishy-smelling steam. There in a stainless steel tray were a bunch of cigars, smelling of fish.

"You see!" cried Captain Van Straaten, "just like magic! Almost anything you want, except a decent corned-beef sandwich, can be had in this way. In time, I will teach you gentlemen to operate the fish synthesizer, and you can come in here and make whatever you desire."

Uncle Mel was really interested in the fish synthesizer. It was the most complicated machine he had ever seen that made bad-tasting food while you waited—and cigars, even! I could see he was very impressed.

"We also have television on board," said Captain Van Straaten, "and radio, a small library, and a collection of phonograph records. The taste of whoever outfitted this boat ran to Spike Jones and modern French organ music. I hope that will suit you. In short, gentlemen, everything you need is here on the *Flying Piggie*. I know you will be very happy."

After saying this, Captain Van Straaten reached inside a jacket and took out a very large revolver. "Please don't be alarmed, gentlemen, but now I must ask you to go quietly to your quarters. It's time for lights out, you know. I regret that I will have to lock you in for the night. Just a formality, you understand. Now, march!"

Captain Van Straaten herded us into the little room with the hammocks. "I'll be letting you out at breakfast time. It's fish flakes and fish milk tomorrow—yummy! Good night." He closed the door and locked it.

· 20 ·

This will never do," said Colonel Ken Krenwinkle.

"No, indeed," said Professor Ambrose McFwain.

"We're prisoners!" said Uncle Mel.

"I don't want fish flakes for breakfast for the rest of my life," I said.

"I think that what Captain Van Straaten is doing is against the law," said Captain Sinbad Weinstein.

"I think we can overpower him and take that revolver away," said Colonel Ken Krenwinkle.

"We promised we wouldn't do that," Uncle Mel said.

"That was before he pulled a gun on us," Colonel Ken Krenwinkle said. "That's very bad manners, and we don't have to treat him like a gentleman after a trick like that."

"But, Colonel," Professor McFwain said, "even if we did overpower him, could we operate this submarine? Suppose we took away his revolver and tied him up. He might be very upset, and he might not be willing to tell us how to operate the boat. Don't forget, we're underwater."

"That's true," Colonel Ken Krenwinkle said. "Captain Sinbad Weinstein, can you operate this submarine?"

"It isn't like any other boat," Captain Sinbad Weinstein said. "Maybe if I had an instruction manual, or if Captain Van Straaten would give me lessons for a week or so . . ."

"In other words, we can't run the boat without Captain Van Straaten, and as long as he's in charge, he'll keep us prisoners," said Uncle Mel.

"That seems to be the case," said Professor Ambrose McFwain.

"But Captain Van Straaten doesn't like being on this boat, really," I said. "He doesn't like it any more than we do. He just wants to keep us on board because he's lonely."

"That's true, Eugene," Professor McFwain said, "but it doesn't alter our predicament."

"Yes, it does," I said. "The only way for us to get off this boat is to take Captain Van Straaten with us. We have to figure out a way to break his curse."

"What Eugene says makes sense," Colonel Ken Krenwinkle said. "That is, assuming there really is a curse, and that Captain Van Straaten isn't just a garden-variety lunatic. But how are we going to break the curse? He has to get to land—and the boat is somehow magically programmed to get no closer than five miles to land. Captain Van Straaten can't swim, and any artificial aid, such as a life-preserver, is technically regarded as a ship under the terms of his curse. I assume that if we swam with him and kept him afloat, then we would be technically regarded as a ship and wouldn't be able to get closer than five miles from shore either."

"The second condition of lifting the curse," Colonel Ken Krenwinkle went on, "would be no problem, of course, if we land in the vicinity of Rochester. I happen to own a restaurant where the best corned-beef sandwiches in the state can be had, a little gourmet place called Fred's Fat Pig."

"You own Fred's Fat Pig?" Uncle Mel and Professor McFwain shouted.

"Yes. I've owned it for years. I own all sorts of things," said Colonel Ken Krenwinkle.

Uncle Mel and Professor Ambrose McFwain looked at Colonel Ken Krenwinkle with admiration.

Captain Sinbad Weinstein spoke, "I think Eugene has hit upon the only solution. We must help Captain Van Straaten get free of his curse. The question is how to do that. I think I may have an idea. It may not work, and it may be dangerous, but it's worth a try. But first, I have to ask him some questions. Let's try and get him to talk to us."

We beat on the walls of the little room with our shoes, and shouted and screamed until we heard Captain Van Straaten's voice over the loudspeaker. "What is it? You woke me up with all that noise!"

"Captain Van Straaten, this is Captain Sinbad Weinstein," Captain Sinbad Weinstein said. "We are considering ways to help you break the curse, and we have to ask you some questions."

"Really?" Captain Van Straaten said. "I'll be right down to let you out. We'll go to the galley and make some fish-cocoa and talk it over."

Captain Van Straaten came to unlock the door

of the crew's quarters wearing a really fancy bathrobe with gold embroidered dragons on it. It was five times as fancy as the bathrobe Professor McFwain had given Uncle Mel.

"Captain Van Straaten," Professor McFwain said, "you can dispense with that ugly revolver. We all agree to give our word to do nothing violent. Besides, we realize that without you to help us we can never get out of this submarine."

"Thank you," said Captain Van Straaten. "I would never have used the gun. It's just that so many crews have run away. Besides the gun is made of hard rubber anyway. It doesn't shoot."

In the galley, Captain Van Straaten served us mugs of hot fish-cocoa. It tasted like fish, of course.

Captain Sinbad Weinstein spoke. "Captain Van Straaten, please tell us exactly what the terms of your curse consist of."

· 21 ·

I'm flattered that you're interested in my story," Captain Van Straaten said, "but did you have to wake me up in the middle of the night to ask me that? Besides, I believe I already told you. I have to get to land, which is next to impossible; and once there, I have to be offered a decent corned-beef sandwich within twenty-four hours, or I have to steal a ship of some sort and put out to sea again."

"We're sorry to have awakened you," Professor McFwain said, "but we think that maybe we can help you—at least we want to."

"That's awfully nice of you," Captain Van Straaten said.

"Now tell us," Captain Sinbad Weinstein said, "exactly how the curse goes. Do you have a copy of it written down somewhere? What are the exact words of the curse?"

"Do you think I need to have the curse written down? I remember every word of it. Of course, it's in Dutch, but I can give you a rough translation. It goes like this:

As punishment for being a no-good, low-down, rotten so-and-so, Captain Seymour Van Straaten is cursed and shall forever sail the sea. No vessel with that miserable skunk on board shall ever float in waters closer than five miles from shore.

Only if that filthy creep can somehow get to land shall this curse be lifted, and then only if some kind soul will offer him a corned-beef sandwich on rye, with cole slaw and a pickle, of good quality within one day of his setting foot on land.

Let the fate of this worthless low-life be a lesson for all who break the sacred code of the sea.

"That's the curse?" Uncle Mel asked.

"Horrible, isn't it?" Captain Van Straaten said.

140

"The curse says 'No vessel shall ever *float* in waters closer than five miles from shore'?" Captain Sinbad Weinstein asked.

"That's what it says," Captain Van Straaten said. "I'm not sure it's good grammar, but that's what it says."

"Tell me," Captain Sinbad Weinstein said, "does this submarine have hydroplanes?"

"Of course, it does," Captain Van Straaten said. "Every submarine has hydroplanes."

"What are hydroplanes?" I asked.

"They're horizontal rudders. The sub uses them to dive and surface," Captain Van Straaten said. "They are rather like wings."

"Exactly!" said Captain Sinbad Weinstein. "And you told me that this submarine can go faster than 100 miles per hour, land speed."

"Oh, much faster," Captain Van Straaten said. "Goodness knows how fast she will go."

"Now," said Captain Sinbad Weinstein, "what would happen if we were to get going really fast on the surface—say, 150 miles per hour?"

"Well, the nose of the boat would rise up out of the water, and she'd sort of skip along—flying almost," Captain Van Straaten said.

"That's called hydroplaning," Captain Sinbad Weinstein said. "In fact, the boat actually

141

turns into a sort of airplane and is not really floating in the water, but skipping along above the surface—the whole hull is out of the water."

"And the curse says . . ." shouted Uncle Mel.

"The curse says floating," said Captain Sinbad Weinstein.

"Fantastic," said Professor McFwain. "Captain Van Straaten, do you think such a thing is possible, and do you think it would release you from the curse?"

"It would be worth a try," said Captain Van Straaten. "Except for one thing."

"And what is that?" Colonel Ken Krenwinkle asked.

"Well, I'd like to know what would happen when we hit the shore going maybe 160 or 170 knots," Captain Van Straaten said. "I expect we'd all be smashed to pieces."

"Not necessarily," said Captain Sinbad Weinstein. "Suppose we headed for a sandy, sloping beach. The nose of the boat is already up in the air. We'd just hydroplane through the shallow water and ride up onto the beach and skid to a stop. The soft sand would help us slow down."

"Unless we hit something hard first," I said.

"Well, the plan is not without risk," said Captain Van Straaten, "but it does seem worth a try. If it doesn't work out, I will just have to float around until I can get another ship. I'm immortal, you know—it goes with the curse."

"But we're not," Uncle Mel said.

"Well, then it's a greater risk for you," said Captain Van Straaten. "I want you all to know that I really appreciate the sacrifice you may be making for me." Then he turned to Captain Sinbad Weinstein and said, "I say let's try it."

"I say let's talk it over some more," I said.

"The next thing to do is have a speed trial," Captain Sinbad Weinstein said. "Captain, let's take her up and see how fast she'll go."

"Excuse me," Uncle Mel said, "but I don't see why we all have to be on board for this landing. Couldn't you cruise around and find *La Forza Materiale* and put us back on board, and then make your high-speed run for shore?"

"I knew it!" shouted the Flying Dutchman. "This is all a trick to get off the *Flying Piggie!* I'm not going to surface, so there! Now get back to your room!" He began waving the pistol about.

"Captain Van Straaten, you have already told us that the gun is made of hard rubber," Colonel Ken Krenwinkle said. "Now, if we promise to stay on board will you try out Captain Sinbad Weinstein's idea?"

"Well, if you all promise . . ." Captain Van Straaten said.

"Of course, we promise," said Colonel Ken Krenwinkle, and then he turned to Uncle Mel. "Sir, I can see you have a lot to learn about adventuring. You will stick this out to the bitter end."

"That's what I'm afraid of," said Uncle Mel.

· 22 ·

Captain Van Straaten took the *Flying Piggie* to the surface to make some speed trials with Captain Sinbad Weinstein. There wasn't room for more than two people in the little cockpit on top of the pig-submarine's back, so the rest of us had to wait down below. We could hear Captain Van Straaten and Captain Sinbad Weinstein shouting and screaming. "Whee!" "Let's go faster!" "Oh, boy!"

It wasn't very pleasant. Inside the submarine all we could feel was a terrible vibration, and all we could hear, except for the excited shouts of the two sea captains, was the roar of the engines.

145

"We're doing 180 knots!" we heard Captain Sinbad Weinstein shout.

"She's lifting! She's lifting!" Captain Van Straaten shouted. "We're airborne! We're flying!"

It felt to us as though the boat was going to rip apart. I felt sort of sick. Uncle Mel *was* sick. Professor McFwain and Colonel Ken Krenwinkle didn't seem too comfortable either. By the end of the speed trial, I was the only one who didn't look green, although I didn't feel exactly wonderful. I was sorry I had had my fish-cocoa.

Captain Van Straaten and Captain Sinbad Weinstein came down the ladder. They were very excited. "We can do it!" Captain Van Straaten said.

"She flies like a bird!" Captain Sinbad Weinstein said.

"Let's take her ashore right now!" Captain Van Straaten said.

"Why not!" said Captain Sinbad Weinstein.

"Don't you think it would be safer to wait for daylight?" Professor McFwain asked.

"There's no need," Captain Sinbad Weinstein said. "The fog has lifted and the night is clear. We can see the shore perfectly. I'll pilot her in from the bridge, and Captain Van Straaten can stay below and keep an eye on the engines. We don't want to run out of speed."

"Really, I don't see why we can't wait for morning," Uncle Mel said.

"Well, there is a reason," Captain Van Straaten said. "Something about the curse I forgot to tell you. You see, I am only able to surface for a few days every seven years. According to my calculations, starting tomorrow at dawn—which is only four hours away—we will have to go under for seven years. Of course, if you don't mind a short wait, we can make our landing seven years from now. I have a Scrabble set and a lot of other games to pass the time."

"Seven years may seem short to you, Captain," Colonel Ken Krenwinkle said, "but it is not short to me. I say let's go for the shore."

"Splendid," said Captain Sinbad Weinstein. "Now who wants to come up and watch from the bridge?"

"I do," I said. I don't know why I said it, except that I really needed some fresh air, and I knew that if I had to stay below during another 180-knot run, I was going to be sick.

"There's no time to lose," said Captain Van Straaten. "Eugene, go up top with Captain Sinbad Weinstein. I'll tend the engines."

"Captain, if this works, you shall have the finest corned-beef sandwich in the world within the hour," Colonel Ken Krenwinkle said.

I went up the ladder with Captain Sinbad Weinstein.

"See that white stretch of shoreline?" he asked me. "That's either a beach, or a concrete embankment. If it is a beach, we should slide right up it, nice as you please."

"What if it's a concrete embankment?" I asked.

"Then we'll be smashed to bits," Captain Sinbad Weinstein said. "But don't worry—I'm almost sure it's a beach." He spoke into a sort of tube that connected to the engine room. "Captain, you may give me full speed whenever you're ready."

The engines screamed, and we started forward. I never went so fast in my life. At first the nose of the *Flying Piggie* cut through the water, making two great mountains of spray on either side, but as we went faster and faster, the nose began to lift up, and the spray began to fall away from the pig-submarine.

"She's lifting! She's lifting!" Captain Sinbad Weinstein shouted.

148

The boat was rocking slightly from side to side. I could feel it losing contact with the water. Then we were sort of bouncing along. I remembered times I had skipped stones over the surface of water—that's what the *Flying Piggie* was doing, hopping along. Each hop was twenty or thirty feet at first; then the hops got longer. At last the motion of the boat became smooth again, except for a terrific vibration from the engines, and I knew we were actually flying over the water.

"Isn't this great, Eugene?" Captain Sinbad Weinstein shouted over the engine noise.

"Can you tell if that's a beach or a concrete wall yet?" I shouted back.

"Not yet," he shouted. "But don't worry—we still have time to turn away if we have to."

"It looks like a wall to me," I shouted.

"It's still too far to tell," Captain Sinbad Weinstein shouted.

"It's a wall! It's a wall!" I shouted.

"It's a beach!" Captain Sinbad Weinstein shouted.

"It's a wall!"

"It's a beach!"

"It's a beach *and* a wall!" I screamed. "It's a beach with a concrete wall running along in front of it!"

"I believe you're right," Captain Sinbad Weinstein said.

"Turn the boat! Turn the boat!" I screamed. I was really scared.

"It's too late for that, Eugene," Captain Sinbad Weinstein said. "If we start to turn now, we'll hit the wall at an angle, and that will be really bad. The only thing we can do is try to go over the wall and onto the beach. We might be able to do that—it depends how high the wall is." He shouted into the speaking tube, "Captain Van Straaten, open her up all the way. We have to clear an obstacle that might be as high as ten feet."

I could hear Captain Van Straaten laughing like a madman through the speaking tube. Suddenly the engines, which had been screaming all along, began to make a noise unlike anything I had ever heard before. I didn't so much hear it as feel it. It was too loud to hear. I felt as though I was inside the noise. The boat surged forward. My hair stood out straight behind me. I felt my nose pressing into my face. My teeth hurt. I felt pressure on my eyeballs. My vision got blurry.

"Now *this* is what I call fast," Captain Sinbad Weinstein said.

I couldn't hear him say it. I just saw him moving his lips, which were distorted by the force of our forward travel.

I could see the wall clearly now. It was solid concrete, and it looked as though it was fifteen or twenty feet high. We were doing 230 knots—over 280 miles per hour!

· 23 ·

This is what a couple of fishermen who were camping out on the beach saw:

The *Flying Piggie,* which the fishermen thought was a gigantic swimming pig, came roaring along at over two hundred miles an hour. It cleared the concrete breakwater by a couple of inches, and belly whopped onto the sandy beach. On the beach it continued to travel at a slightly reduced speed—maybe a hundred and seventy-five miles per hour. It traveled the width of the beach, still losing momentum, and was not doing more than sixty when it crossed State Highway 18. Then it cut

152

down sixty-four trees of all sizes, slid across an access road, and came to rest, only slightly damaged, in the parking lot of Fred's Fat Pig.

Captain Sinbad Weinstein and I were fine. We had just held on to the edge of the cockpit. The people below had been tossed around quite a bit, and the inside of the sub was a mess—but nobody was hurt.

Fred's Fat Pig was open all night, so there were some cooks and waitresses inside, but there were no customers in the place. The waitresses recognized Colonel Ken Krenwinkle and didn't seem especially surprised at having a giant pig crash into the parking lot. They knew all about Colonel Ken Krenwinkle's hobby of motor-vehicle hunting and probably thought the *Flying Piggie* had something to do with that.

Colonel Ken Krenwinkle ordered a corned-beef sandwich on rye, with coleslaw and a pickle, for the Flying Dutchman, who gleefully ate it with tartar sauce. Uncle Mel and Professor McFwain had a few dozen hamburgers to celebrate our safe landing.

Colonel Ken Krenwinkle telephoned his driver to come and pick everyone up. Professor McFwain was taken back to the fat men's clothing factory. Uncle Mel and I were taken back to

153

the motel. Captains Van Straaten and Sinbad Weinstein were going to stay at Colonel Ken Krenwinkle's house. We were all going to meet again the next day at Fred's Fat Pig to have a celebration and discuss our adventure.

· 24 ·

Captain Sinbad Weinstein and Captain Van Straaten had become good friends. They decided to convert the *Flying Piggie* into a restaurant and become partners with Colonel Ken Krenwinkle in running it as part of Fred's Fat Pig.

Colonel Ken Krenwinkle was delighted with the idea. He also offered Uncle Mel a job in a new company he wanted to start, which would make all kinds of fast foods, cigars, and other things out of fish, and sell them from vending machines in bus stations, bowling alleys, and other places like that. Uncle Mel took the job, which meant he'd be coming back to Rochester often to see his new friends. He said that sometimes I could come with him.

Professor McFwain applied for a patent on a toy pig that could swim through the water at 260 miles per hour. You've seen them—they're the most popular swimming pool toy since the inflatable shark.

The professor says that he's going to use some of the proceeds from his invention to mount an expedition to find Big Belly, the fabled giant horse of the Arctic Circle. I'm going with him. He says I'm the best assistant he's ever had.

I'm thinking about becoming a professional monster-hunter myself when I grow up.